Other books by Craig Davidson

RUST AND BONE (stories)
A savage world populated by fighting dogs, prizefighters, sex addicts, and gamblers. "Smudges the line between comedy and horror, cruelty and mercy. His remarkable stories are challenging and upsetting, but never boring." —Chuck Palahniuk, author of *Fight Club*

THE FIGHTER (a novel)
Set in the violent world of illegal bare-knuckle boxing, *The Fighter* unflinchingly captures that world's colourful denizens, its bleakness, its bracing and bloody violence. "*The Fighter* is an essential novel, destined for cult status at the very least." —Irvine Welsh, author of *Trainspotting* and *Filth*

SARAH COURT (a novel)
Ask yourself: How well do you know your neighbours? How well do you know your own family? Ultimately, how well do you know yourself? How deeply do the threads of your own life entwine with those around you? Do you ever really know how tightly those threads are knotted?

CATARACT CITY (a novel)
Owen and Duncan both dream of escape from Cataract City, a longing made more urgent by a near-death incident in childhood. But in adulthood their paths diverge, and as Duncan, the less privileged, falls into the town's underworld, he and Owen become reluctant adversaries at opposite ends of the law. Shortlisted for the Scotiabank Giller Prize.

PRECIOUS CARGO (memoir)
One morning in 2008, desperate and impoverished and living in a one-room basement apartment while trying unsuccessfully to write, Davidson plucked a flyer out of his mailbox that read, "Bus Drivers Wanted." That was the first step towards an unlikely new career . . . "Craig Davidson's new memoir reveals poignant truths about his year as a Calgary school-bus driver. . . . a sweet and often funny story about [Davidson's] bond with the five children on his route." —*Calgary Herald*

THE SATURDAY NIGHT GHOST CLUB

CRAIG DAVIDSON

Alfred A. Knopf Canada   Toronto

PUBLISHED BY ALFRED A. KNOPF CANADA

Copyright © 2018 Craig Davidson

Published in 2018 by Alfred A. Knopf Canada, a division of Penguin Random House Canada Limited, Toronto. Distributed in Canada by Penguin Random House Canada Limited, Toronto.

www.penguinrandomhouse.ca

Grateful acknowledgment is made for permission to reproduce the following: "The brain is wider than the sky" by Emily Dickinson, from *The Poems of Emily Dickinson*, edited by Thomas H. Johnson, Cambridge, Mass.: The Belknap Press of Harvard University Press, Copyright © 1951, 1955 by the President and Fellows of Harvard College. Copyright © renewed 1979, 1983 by the President and Fellows of Harvard College. Copyright © 1914, 1918, 1919, 1924, 1929, 1930, 1932, 1935, 1937, 1942, by Martha Dickinson Bianchi. Copyright © 1952, 1957, 1958, 1963, 1965, by Mary L. Hampson. Reprinted by permission.

Library and Archives Canada Cataloguing in Publication

Davidson, Craig, 1976–, author
The Saturday night ghost club : a novel / Craig Davidson.

Issued in print and electronic formats.
ISBN 978-0-7352-7482-2
eBook ISBN 978-0-7352-7483-9

I. Title.

PS8607.A79S38 2018   C813'.6   C2018-900088-0
                                             C2018-900089-9

Book design by Five Seventeen

Cover image: (abandoned house) © Ed Freeman / Stone Collection / Getty Images

Printed and bound in the United States of America

10 9 8 7 6 5 4 3 2 1

Penguin
Random House
KNOPF CANADA

To Nicholas,
With all the love in my body.

The Brain—is wider than the Sky—
For—put them side by side—
The one the other will contain
With ease—and You beside—

The Brain is deeper than the sea—
For—hold them—Blue to Blue—
The one the other will absorb—
As Sponges—Buckets—do—

The Brain is just the weight of God—
For—Heft them—Pound for Pound—
And they will differ—if they do—
As Syllable from Sound—

—*Emily Dickinson*, 632

Memory is another word for story,
and nothing is more unreliable.

—*Ann-Marie MacDonald,*
Fall on Your Knees

The ———————
SATURDAY NIGHT
GHOST CLUB

1.

MONSTERS

Most people believe the human brain is solid. They imagine a loaf of bread soaked in gelatin: you can hack off quivering slices, same as you would with a Jell-O mould at a family picnic. But the truth is, the brain's texture is more like toothpaste. Brain matter will squeeze through a keyhole. In cases of severe cranial swelling, surgeons use a drill—I prefer the RA-II, a Korean model: 30,000rpm, with silicone hand-grips for comfort—to bore into the skull. If the swelling cannot be stopped, the living brain will project from the hole in an inverted funnel. This is called a "coning," and it marks an end.

Most people also believe the brain is grey. Its cells are called grey matter, after all, and isn't that how the organ looks in horror flicks: a slaty walnut floating in a jar of formaldehyde in some mad scientist's lab? But a sheathed brain is bracingly pink. The tissue only turns grey once the cerebrospinal sac has been perforated, once the air hits it. When a brain cones, the tissue changes colour; traceries of ash thread through that bubble-gum pink as a million thoughts flicker and die.

People think neurosurgeons cut into brains with a scalpel. Another myth. How can you carve tooth-paste? An infant's brain matter is even less substantial than an adult's, like pancake batter. I operate with a sucker wand, a tool that is exactly as it sounds. As I investigate the runnels of a patient's brain, it grips me that something unforgivingly solid—my wand—is moving through something ephemeral, dreamlike: a patient's memories. Though I work carefully and with a keen knowledge of the cerebral topography, my wand remains a beast blundering through fields of budding shoots. If I trample something critical, the patient may awaken lacking a vital memory. That one where they gazed into the sky as a child wondering how a star might taste, settling on breathtaking win-tergreen. The smell of their newborn daughter's scalp, or that haunting tingle on their lips following their first kiss.

I navigate the storerooms of a patient's consciousness, passing memories in their golden vaults, my wand clumsily bayoneting—it often seems—the pink jelly that holds everything the patient is or will ever be. Hard as I try not to disturb the furniture, things happen. I am forced to accept these tragic outcomes, for the same reason that the patients on my table must accept their own lot: we are only human, a condition of perpetual uncertainty and failure.

The brain is the seat of memory, and memory is a tricky thing. At base level, memories are stories—and sometimes these stories we tell allow us to carry on. Sometimes stories are the best we can hope for. They help us to simply get by, while deeper levels of our consciousness slap bandages on wounds that hold the power to wreck us. So we tell ourselves that the people we love closed their eyes and slipped painlessly away from us. That our personal failures are the product of external forces rather than unfixable weaknesses. That we were too damn good for the rat-assed bastards who jilted us, anyway. Tell yourself these stories long enough and you will discover they have a magical way of becoming facts.

But a secret can be hidden from everyone save its holder, and the brain is not only a storyteller, it is a truth-seeking organ. If the stories we tell are no more than an overlay, the equivalent of six feet of caliche covering a pool of toxic sludge, something's bound to bubble up, right? And the most awful truths will do so in the darkest hours of night, when we're most vulnerable.

If you bury those secrets so deep that you forget they ever happened, okay, maybe you've beat the devil. But the truth is a bloodhound. That's something I can tell you with certainty. The truth is that abandoned dog following you over sea and land, baying from barren clifftops, never tiring and never quitting, forever pining after you—and the day will come when that dog is on your porch, scratching insistently at your door, forcing you to claim it once again.

i.

As a boy, I believed in monsters.

I was convinced that if I said "Bloody Mary" in front of a mirror, a hideous witch-woman would reach through the glass with nails sharp as splinters. I considered it a fact that the Devil lingered at shadowy crossroads and went to dance halls in disguise, where he'd ask the prettiest girl to dance and reel her across the floor while spectators stood terror-stricken at the sight of the Devil's goatish shanks, until the girl fainted dead away and the Unclean One vanished in a puff of brimstone.

There was no falsehood I wouldn't swallow, no quilt of lies you couldn't drape over my all-too-gullible shoulders. But for a boy like me—chubby, freckled, awkward; growing up in a city where the erection of a new Kmart occasioned our mayor to announce, "This marks a wondrous new chapter in our town's history"—imagination was my greatest asset. Not to mention my defence against a foe worse than the most fearsome monster: loneliness.

My ally against that foe was my uncle Calvin. If I told him there was a bottomless pit in my basement, he'd say, "Tell me, Jake, is the air denser around the mouth of the pit than in other areas of the basement?" Cocking an eyebrow: "Do ominous growling sounds emanate from this pit of yours?"

Uncle C was the ideal nursemaid for my paranoid fantasies. His knowledge of urban legends and folk-lore was encyclopedic—with the added bonus that he seemed to consider most of it true.

"Hey," he'd say, "did you know there are crocodiles living in the sewers of our fair city? The poor suckers get smuggled up from Florida by dumb tourists. Sure, they're cute as a bug's ear when they're six inches long.

But when they grow up and get nippy? *Ba-whooosh*, down the porcelain mistake eraser. They get fat 'n' sassy down there in the pipes, where there's plenty to eat if you're not choosy. Every year a couple of sanitation department workers get gobbled up by sewer crocs. The press bottles it up, unscrupulous snakes that they are, but it's a fact you can set your watch to."

Uncle C would fiddle with the beads of his bracelet—each an ornate pewter Cthulhu head, mouths and eye sockets sprouting tentacles—and offer a wistful sigh. "And *that*, Jake, is why owning a pet is a big responsibility."

Once, when I was six or seven, I became convinced a monster lived in my closet. I told my dad, who did what 99 percent of adults do when their child makes this claim: he flung my closet door open, rattled coat hangers and shoved shoeboxes aside, making a Broadway production of it. "See? No monsters, Jake."

But monsters make themselves scarce when adults are around, only to slither back after dark. Every kid knew this to be an unshakable fact.

Uncle C arrived for dinner that night, as usual— Mom invited him every Sunday. He got an inkling of my worry as I sat picking at my Salisbury steak.

"What's the matter, hombre?"

"We have an unwanted visitor in a closet, apparently," Mom informed him.

"But we've established that there's no monster," my father said. "Right, buddy?"

"Ah," said Uncle C. "I have some expertise in this area. Sam, with your permission?"

Mom turned to my father and said, "*Sam*," in the tone of voice you'd use to calm a jittery horse.

"Of course, Cal, as you like," my father said.

My uncle pedalled home to his house, returning ten minutes later with a tool box. Once we were in my bedroom he motioned to the closet. "I take it this is its lair?"

I nodded.

"Closets are a favourite haunt of monsters," my uncle explained. "Most are harmless, even good-tempered, if they have enough dust bunnies and cobwebs to eat. Do you clean your closet?"

I assured him that it was hardly ever tidied unless my mother forced the chore on me.

"Good, let them feast. If they get too hungry they'll crawl over to your clothes hamper and eat holes in your underwear. No need to check the seat of your drawers for confirmation, as I can see by your expression that yours have indeed met this cruel fate."

Calvin cracked the tool box and pulled out an instrument—one that today I'd recognize as a stud finder.

"It's a monster tracer," he said, running it over the closet walls, making exploratory taps with his knuckles. "There are token traces of ectoplasm," he said in the voice of a veteran contractor. "Monster slime, in layman's terms. What does this monster look like?"

"Hairy in some parts, slimy in others."

"What's its shape? Like a snake, or a blob?"

"A blob. But it can stretch, too, so it can look like a snake if it wants."

"We're dealing with a hairy, slimy blob with uncanny stretching capacities." He gripped his chin. "Sounds like a Slurper Slug. They're common around these parts."

"A slug?"

"Correct, but we're not talking your garden-variety slug." He laughed—actually, he exclaimed *ha-ha*. "A little paranormal humour for you, Jake my boy. These peculiar and particularly gross slugs infest closets and crawl spaces. You haven't been keeping anything tasty in your closet, have you?"

"That's where I put my Halloween candy."

"Slurper Slug, then, guaranteed. They're not dangerous, just revolting. They could make a mortician barf his biscuits. If you let one hang around he'll call his buddies and before long you've got an infestation on your hands."

He rooted through his tool box for a pouch of fine red powder. "This is cochineal, made from the crushed shells of beetles. It's used in containment spells."

He laid down a line of powder in the shape of a keyhole:

"This," he said, pointing to the circle, "is the trap. The Slurper Slug will traipse up this path, see, which gets narrower and narrower until the Slug gets stuck in the Circle of No Return. There it will turn black as night and hard as rock. Now, you'll have to pull one hair out of your head to bait the slug trap."

I plucked a single strand, which my uncle laid softly in the trap.

"Go ask your mom if she has any chocolate chips."

I went down to the kitchen to find my folks engaged in a hushed conversation. My father's shoulders were vibrating like twin tuning forks.

"Chocolate chips, huh?" Mom said in a Susie-Cheerleader voice. "I've only got butterscotch."

By the time I got back, the closet was shut. My uncle instructed me to lay a trail of butterscotch chips along the door.

"The sweetness will draw that Slug out of hiding. Now listen, Jake, and listen carefully. If you peek inside the closet, the spell will be broken. Under no circumstances can it be opened until tomorrow morning. No matter the sounds you may hear dribbling through this door, you must leave it closed. Do you swear this to me?"

"Yes, I promise."

"By the Oath of the White Mage, do you swear it?"

When I admitted I didn't know that oath, he stuck out his little finger. "The pinkie variety will suffice."

I linked my finger with his and squeezed.

"Cross your heart and hope to die?"

"Stick a needle in my eye," I said solemnly.

I awoke to sunlight streaming through the window. I crept to the closet and opened it. Just as Uncle C had said, the keyhole was now only a circle and in the middle sat an object that was dark as night and hard as rock.

My uncle was taking off his boots in the front hall when I stormed downstairs.

"The trap worked!" I told him, dragging him up the stairs to show him the blackened slug.

"Pick it up," he said. "It may still be a little warm but it won't burn you."

Queasy warmth pulsed off the slug, or so it felt to me.

"It's not every day that you can hold a monster in your palm, is it, Jake?"

That lump of obsidian would rest on my nightstand for years. Then one day I noticed it sitting between my Junior Sleuths magnifying glass and a dog-eared reissue of Stephen King's *Carrie*, the one with the art deco cover. Opening the drawer, I swept the volcanic rock inside, embarrassed that I'd once been fear-struck by anything so infantile as a snot-ball slug in my closet. . . .

An hour later I took it out and put it back where it belonged.

2.

THE SPIRIT PHONE

What follows is an account, as I choose to remember it, of my twelfth year on this planet—the summer of the Saturday Night Ghost Club. Uncle C called the inaugural meeting, and in addition to him, our membership roll was tiny: Billy Yellowbird, Lexington Galbraith and me. Later on Dove Yellowbird became the club's lone female member.

The club convened in Niagara Falls. Cataract City, as we locals call it. A place stuck in time. The shop awnings are '70s-era candy-stripes, and the row houses have tarpaper roofs. The rooms in every motel down the strip—flops with names like the Lovers' Nest and the Honeydew Inn—smell of burnt dust and carpet powder, and the duvets look like somebody's grandma's sofa covers. Nothing ever gets torn down in Cataract City. Buildings collapse like woolly mammoths sucked lamenting into a tar pit, and afterwards, the spot where that dilapidated house or shop stood remains barren. In most towns, things change. Vacant lots become parking lots, or gentrification hits and they become tapas restaurants and dog grooming salons. But where I come from those weedy lots become part of the scenery. People would miss them if they were gone.

Cataract City is perma-tacky, but you come to love it the way you'd love an ugly dog with a sweet disposition. The population swells when the tourist tide washes in each summer—that spree-spending, sunburnt horde—but they clear out come late August, leaving nothing but their money. Just enough babies are born at the Niagara Gen to compensate for those who are lost in the retirement castles strung down Dunn Street. A lot of the guys I grew up with roam the streets they were born on, living a block from their childhood homes. *Cradle to grave* could be Cataract City's unofficial motto. Some days I peer out the window of my glittery Toronto apartment tower—everything glitters in my part of town; at the first sign of tarnish the wrecking ball starts to swing—and spot that distant landfall across Lake Ontario. The city of my birth is only a few hours down the highway if traffic holds steady, and a part of me will always belong there.

My parents still live in their bungalow on Belmont Road. My room is as I left it: the *Dead Alive* poster on the wall and the stack of *Fangoria*s on the bookshelf, under a shrunken skull that Uncle C told me he'd bartered from a Peruvian headshrinker, but replicas of which I later found filling a wire bin—three dozen miniaturized specimens—in the Ripley's Believe It or Not gift shop on Clifton Hill. I spent my childhood within the confines of that house, or haunting a few lonely bolt-holes around town where I wouldn't be harassed by lads whose chief pleasure was torturing introspective bookish sorts like me.

Back then, the world had jaws that could grip at any time. That tree branch scratching my window at night? That was the fingernail of a vampire roused from the catacombs beneath the Lundy's Lane cemetery. Its face pale as lamplight, its eyes twin craters burrowed into its skull, its ragged nail *scriiiiiiiitch*-ing the glass. The rustling of dead leaves in the eaves-troughs was the scuttling of rats in the walls. Not just any old rats: bloated hulks with tails like cherry licorice whips. They skittered behind the drywall on needle-nail feet, harvesting the insulation to build a nest for their mother, the queen, who was the size of a trash can, squatting behind our water tank. The queen had suckled on nameless goo seeping from a cracked drum at the city dump before squeezing through the dryer vent to give birth to a brood of squealing rat-lings. Before long they'd chew through my bedroom wall and pour out in a chittering tide of rancid fur and teeth the colour of stained ivory, and those pink coiling tails. . . .

Looking back, it's a wonder I got any sleep at all.

Can't say I get much these days, either. I work at St. Michael's Hospital in downtown Toronto. Neurosurgery unit. I'm a BCB—a "Big City Blade"—a sobriquet coined by one of the more egotistical members of my fraternity. My job obliges me to enter the operating theatre, where I cut into the human brain. Whenever I bisect a patient's scalp and remove a scalloped window of skull to assay the knotty web of blood vessels braiding across a brain's surface—a venous geography individual to each patient, like a fingerprint—I am beset by a passing but intense fear that collects in my mouth, bitter as chewed aspirin.

There was a time, years ago, when I'd drive all the way home after a gruelling operation and take my folks out to Lucky's Steakhouse. If I was feeling nostalgic—or if the procedure had gone badly—I'd sleep in my old bed. My feet would dangle over the edge, but the sheets smelled as they did when I was a boy. Mom hung them on the line to dry, so they held different scents from season to season: budding blossoms in spring, honeysuckle in summer, a hint of wood-smoke come autumn. I'd lie with the moonlight angling through the backyard maple to cast a fretwork of shadows on the wall and remember the ghost of my old fears, although I no longer saw the shadows as the skeletal hands of a beast come to claim my soul.

i.

That summer of my twelfth year had a rough start when Percy Elkins chucked a firecracker at my head after the last bell of the school year.

We'd once been friends, Percy and me. When he'd first arrived in town, Percy sought me out. New kids usually did. I'd shown Percy those secret spots that were my own back then: the pool of still river under the train trestle teeming with whiskery catfish, the ice caves along the escarpment where the water trickled into the rock. In time, Percy found cooler guys to pal around with. I was used to that.

But then Percy became my tormentor. Shooting spitballs at the back of my neck, so wet I felt like I was being hit with warm cottage cheese. Tripping me during wind sprints in gym class. Squashing a wad of grape Bubblicious in my hair, two whole cubes, so much gum he looked like a wrathful chipmunk in the moment before the act. It took half a jar of peanut butter to get it out, and my scalp reeked of Skippy for a week. Percy cheerfully led the schoolyard in a rousing rendition of "Fatty Fatty Two by Four"—who, as everyone knows, couldn't get through the bathroom door, so he did it on the floor, licked it up and et cetera. No longer could I go back to my old cherished spots for fear he'd hunt me down there.

Percy was different from the other boys who picked on me. So long as I took the abuse with a chin-dimpled, verge-of-tears look and didn't fight back, they usually laid off. Percy felt no such pity. One of his go-to torments was to jam a pencil down the cleft of his unnaturally sweaty ass and chase me around with it—daring me to stop him, his eyes assuring me he could cook up something much worse than a Pink Pearl clammy with butt-sweat if I gave him a reason to. Thing was, Percy was a shrimp with teeth that bucked like shingles on a cedar-shake roof. Judging by size alone, I should've creamed him. But Percy was scary in a way that shrunk me to the size of an ant.

When I noticed him stalking across the soccer field after last bell on that final day, skirting the baseball diamond with his predatory lope—the unsettling stride of a Robert Crumb cartoon character come to life—really, I should have realized what was in store. But it was the final day of school. Surely even a bacterium as vile as Percy wouldn't bother wasting a minute of such a glorious day abusing me.

A heavy-faced boy named Terry Vreeland mooned along after Percy. The Vreelands were a snake-bitten clan who lived out near the old dog track. Once, when I was getting a drink from the fountain outside the teachers' lounge, I overheard the public health nurse telling the gym teacher, Mrs. Fonseca, that the Vreeland children were "hair-lice and tapeworm recidivists." This mystery only added to Terry's menace. Now Terry handed something to Percy. Percy fiddled with whatever it was, smiling chummily at me as if to say, *Jake, my friend! All that horrible stuff I said about you? I didn't mean it, honestly!*

He swung his arm in an underhand motion, like he was rolling a bowling ball down the lane. Something arced towards me—

Bang!

The firecracker exploded in front of my eyes, scorching my retinas. I screamed—or I think I did, but my ears were ringing—and I fell backwards, my sinuses burning with gunpowder.

The next thing I heard was Terry Vreeland's whinnying laughter. *A-heee! A-heee!* The most beautiful sound on earth, as it meant my eardrums hadn't ruptured. My sightlines were wonky, the edges blown out, whiteness dancing at the edges of my vision. I staggered to my feet and tried to run, but the treads of my sneakers, nearly bald after a spring spent running away from encounters not half so frightening as this one, couldn't grip the sun-torched grass. Percy kicked me in the ass and sent me sprawling.

I watched as Percy touched his lighter's flame to the wick of a Black Cat firecracker no bigger than a pencil stub. I brought my arms up to shield my face . . . but for a long moment, nothing happened. When I peeked out between my fingers, I saw Percy staggering around clutching the back of his skull. The firecracker dropped between his legs and went off harmlessly, kicking up a puff of dirt.

Then I saw that Percy's hands were painted bright red. He turned woozily. The wispy blond hair at the back of his head was wet and heavy with blood. A girl stood twenty yards from him with her hips shot to one side, holding a skateboard by its trucks. Her free hand clutched a rock.

"You . . . *bitch*," Percy spat. "You threw a rock at me."

"Congratulations on solving the big case, Sherlock." The girl jutted her chin at Terry Vreeland. "You didn't even need the help of your trusty associate, Fatson."

Percy's eyes took on a shrewd, calculating sheen.

"Terr," he said almost pleasantly. "Let's rip her jaw off."

He and Terry advanced towards the girl . . . who stood her ground, bouncing the stone in her palm as if testing its weight. It was the size of a robin's egg and speckled with black dots.

"I played baseball for five years," she said casually.

Percy's head tilted like a dog hearing a whistle.

"On the boys' team," she clarified. "Pitcher. Coach told me I was too wild. I'd put one right down the pipe for a strike, then the next one would sail five feet over the catcher's head. But I threw hard. Coach liked that." She scuffed the dirt with her shoe the same way a pitcher did on the mound. "If you take another step, I'm gonna chuck this. Can't say at who, but I'm leaning towards you," she told Percy evenly, "because your teeth need fixing, and even the dentists in this fly-strip of a town could do a better job than Mother Nature did."

She followed this with a shrug. "There's a fifty percent chance I miss. Probably more than fifty when you consider the tension of the moment."

Her fingers curled around the stone in a split-fingered fastball grip. There was a bright lunacy in her eyes. A look that said, *I can foresee the future and you idiots ain't in it.* Percy must've seen it, too: it was kissing cousin to the look in his own eyes.

"You fight dirty." Percy's lip curled. "A dirty fighter, chucking rocks."

I wanted to chime in that Percy was hardly a paragon of fair fighting, tossing firecrackers at unsuspecting people's faces, but kept my mouth shut.

"It's a *looooong* summer," Percy told her. "Be seeing you."

Once he and Terry left, the girl helped me up. I wanted to thank her but my tongue lay stunned in my mouth. I couldn't understand why she'd put herself on the line for me.

"Percy'll need stitches," is what I blurted out at last.

"Is that his name? Fits him. Why do you give a shit about that?"

"I don't care at all. He's a . . ."

"Piss-stain?" she offered. "Bag-munch? The Dynamic Dr. Douchenstein?"

Again, I couldn't speak. Something about this girl made my critical faculties go haywire.

"That's my good deed for the decade." She threw her skateboard over her shoulder the way a lumberjack shoulders an axe. "Be seeing you."

ii.

When I was a kid my father used to come home with blood on his knuckles—which was weird, considering he was a banker.

Dad was the youngest of a brood, the Bakers, who lived in a rambling house on Sofia Street on the east side of Niagara Falls. My grandparents had one daughter, Julia, followed by seven sons. John and Jeffry, then Allen, then Theodore—whom everyone called Teddy—then the twins Billy and Bobby, then Sam, my father. After that, Grandma said the one daughter would suffice.

The day Percy threw that firecracker at me, I went home and scrubbed my face. Pinpricks of blood wept from little holes in my cheeks. Bits of paper had penetrated my skin deep enough to cut me open, like a thousand tiny paper cuts.

I was sitting on the sofa watching *The Beachcombers* when my father got home. The cuts had clotted up enough by then to blend in with my freckles.

"How's tricks, kiddo? Wait, have you been crying?" My father never got on me for crying, probably figuring I had more reason to do so than other kids. "Missing your teachers already?"

"Nope. I mean, nope I haven't been crying."

"You ought to wear sunblock, son-o'-mine. With your complexion, you'll be burnt to a cinder by the middle of July."

I didn't tell him about the firecracker. He would have launched into a sermon about the need to stick up for myself. Or worse, he'd do something crazy like head to Percy's house and challenge his father to a fight.

My father's clan, the Bakers, were known around Cataract City as "the Breakers": nose-breakers, ball-breakers, promise-breakers, law-breakers, occasionally heartbreakers. It wasn't just the brothers, either: my aunt Julia could throw a wicked overhand right.

I'd heard about nights where the brothers would get vipered up on Comrade Popov's potato vodka— $2.75 a gallon at Wedge Discount Liquors across the river—and pound down on some ill-lit tavern like the hammers of hell. They'd stir up shit with another of the city's brotherhoods, the Murphys or Carrolls or Specks, or else some soldiers on furlough from CFB Petawawa, and before long be out on the sidewalk swinging fists. The Baker boys were happy to take five licks to give one back. It was easy to spot a Breaker around town: look for the squashed noses and smiles that resembled a windblown picket fence. But my uncles and aunt did smile, a lot. They were great lovers of life. They also happened to be masochists. My father used to say, *We're Irish, Jake, which means heredity carries us halfway to madness smack out of the womb.* Short of a stake through the heart, it was all but impossible to put a Baker down in a fight.

And I'd heard about those fights. By all accounts, my father and his brothers fought like a pack of wolverines. They came at you as one entity, a crazed unit spiked with long bony limbs, the air surrounding it perfumed with flammable fumes. If you slugged that mass, it might go down—part of it would, at least—but the whole would drag its fallen portion up, one part momentum and two parts wrath, unhinged and angrier, the fight jacked all through it.

The Breakers fought hard but fair. No rabbit punches, no fishhooks, no crotch shots. When an opponent cried "*no mas*" they were pleased to stop. They'd shake your hand with a dopey adrenalized smile on their faces, then invite you back into the bar for a drink.

"There's something stupidly thrilling to a tussle, Jake," my father would tell me. "Afterwards, the stars are brighter than you've ever known. The vodka . . . we called it fight juice. It's as if a mad genius bottled up a bunch of ghastly spirits, put a cap on them, then waited for us idiots to come along and chug those evil genies down."

My mother dragged my dad away from that life. Mom hailed from different stock. Her own mother was a social worker, and her father the branch manager of the ScotiaBank on Stanley Avenue. My mother and her brother, Calvin, were the polar opposite of the Bakers: bookish, musical, pacifist. Mom played first-string flute in high school band. As a young woman, she took part in an animal-rights protest at Land of Oceans, our city's cut-rate SeaWorld, only to get pegged with a beer bottle chucked from a passing pickup, the thrower hollering, "Go get laid, ya cold fish!" The bottle opened the skin above her eyebrow and the cut healed into a scar resembling a bone fishhook.

She met my father at the Bonnevilla House. More accurately, they met outside it. My mother's teenage years had been, in her eyes, sheltered—so at twenty-one she found herself at the Bonny House with some more adventurous of her friends from the university where she was studying sociology.

It happened as such things do. A pair of eyes meeting across the smoky air. My father's interest was easy to nail down, my mother's much less so. At the time, Dad wore a cracked leather jacket and his hair in a mullet, the classic "Niagara Waterfall." His cheekbone, cut up in a recent tussle, had a Band-Aid flapping off it.

"I looked like a bargain-bin Fonzie," he told me. *"Eeeeh, sit on it!"*

"There was just something about him," Mom would say in response to this, as if to indicate the attraction existed beyond rational explanation. "His eyes didn't fit with the rest of him. There was an intelligence to them. A kindness."

"Your mother is a tireless turd polisher," was my father's official position on the matter.

That night the brothers got drunk, picked a fight, and scrapped outside the bar. Afterwards, the rest of them went back inside to drink away their lumps. My father lingered under the glow of the parking lot's light stanchion; he was cut and didn't want to drip blood on the Bonny's parquet floor. Mom came out. Neither remembers exactly what was said, but it must have been enough.

Mom dated him on the sly. Was she actually falling for this scruffy, scabby-knuckled boy?

What did my father do? Hustled pool. Sharked the rubes at dollar-limit stud poker in the utility shed behind the Knights of Columbus baseball diamond. Drove a delivery truck for Gorson Bros. Furniture Closeouts when his older brother begged off sick. That wasn't a life my mother would willingly align herself with, and it wasn't her job to change Sam Baker.

"Thus, she dumped me." Dad would snap his fingers, relaying the story to me. "Dropped my ass like a bad habit."

When Mom stopped answering his calls, my father agonized as only a love-starved young man could. He'd lost the love of his life. A life overhaul was in order. He hacked off the mullet, shaved the scruff, bought the best suit he could afford—from the Rowe Funeral Home, as it happened; the mortician was eager to part with a tweedy number that had recently draped a stiff whose measurements matched my father's—then marched into my grandfather's bank and asked for a job.

My grandfather knew about the notorious Bakers but his heart was rich with Christian benevolence. He gave my father a teller's job. Turned out Dad was a whiz with numbers, a talent that had lain dormant through all the drinking and carousing. Mom saw he was trying to make good, and little by little she thawed.

They got hitched at the Two Hearts Wedding Chapel on Stanley Avenue and settled into the house I'd grow up in. My father was promoted to assistant manager. Mom got a job with the Children's Aid Society . . . then she missed her period, peed on a stick and up popped the "+" sign. After some tears and a frank discussion they decided to keep me.

People say a hellion can go one of two ways upon the birth of a child. One, the responsibility wrecks him and he reverts to his shit-disturbing ways. Two, he separates so completely from his old self that it's impossible to believe he could ever have been so wild.

My father split that particular atom. Most days he was the second type of man, but every so often . . .

One night I stirred from sleep at three in the morning and crept downstairs to see my mother sitting stock-still on the chesterfield. A taxi pulled into the driveway. The front window flooded with headlamp-glow, illuminating her in her housecoat.

My father staggered out of the cab with blood gleaming on his knuckles. He stumbled in, smelling like he'd toppled into a vat of sour mash. Mom met him squarely in the hallway. A sharp *snak!* as her open palm laced his cheek.

"I'm sorry, Cece," my father said. "My brothers, John and Al and Jeff . . . just a few beers but . . . Jesus."

He shook his head and snorted, a sound of sheer disgust.

"My hands have gone soft counting other people's money, Cece. It wells up. It *hurts*. Physically, in my bones. It wells and wells and it *wells*—"

"You better quit all this, Sam. Goddamn it, I mean it."

The pleading went out of him then. Snuffed like a trembling flame.

"Okay, Cecilia. I will, I will."

Fatherhood steadily changed my dad. It wasn't that the iron was ripped out of his spine. Rather, that same iron was reallocated to other parts of him where it could do more good. He quit hard liquor. *Cut off his drinking legs*, as they say around town. By the time I hit ten he'd stopped coming home bloody-knuckled. And he never even taught me how to throw a punch.

iii.

This city is haunted by ghosts.

Uncle C used to say this, though not to scare me. He'd say it with a cocked eyebrow and an inscrutable smile, a merry jester beckoning me to embark on a grand adventure.

Uncle C was my mother's older brother, though you'd never guess it. Mom was pragmatic, clear-sighted. Ever since I'd known him, Uncle C had been a dreamer. He was an expert in lore of unspecified worth, a believer in things that went bump in the night, a self-professed seer between the worlds of the living and the dead. He was a conspiracy theorist of the highest order, and, as a result, just about the best uncle a boy like me could ask for.

He was incredibly tall, or so he seemed back then. (I realize now that, at six foot three, he was not quite the fairytale giant who exists in my memory.) He moved awkwardly, as though threads were attached to his limbs, trailing up to a novice puppeteer. He claimed this was the result of his nerves failing to stretch down to his toes and fingertips. This, his further claim went, was a common affliction of the Watusi tribesmen in Africa, who were so tall that their heads brushed the branches of the baobab trees. The Watusis were poor warriors, unable to hurl a spear accurately, and were frequently carried off into the veldt by enterprising tigers. His long horse-like face was prematurely seamed—he would have been in his late thirties that summer—his green eyes set in a fine net of wrinkles. His hair had turned bone-white before I was born and he wore it past his shoulders. With that hair and his elongated limbs and joints that bulged like knots in a rope, he reminded me of the gnarled cypress trees that thrive in Floridian swamps.

Odd duck. That was my father's term for the Uncle Cs of this world. And my uncle *was* weird, but not in a threatening way. He didn't collect his urine in Mason jars or dress his cats in sailor outfits and have them re-enact *HMS Pinafore* or waltz around his living room with an old mannequin torso he picked up at the city dump. Uncle C was harmless, as I've found to be the case with most odd ducks. As far as I was concerned, there was nothing wrong with being an odd duck. I figured some people have edges that don't allow them to slot neatly into the holes society expects them to fit into, that was all.

My uncle owned a shop, the Occultorium, at the top of Clifton Hill. The name was spelled out in Gothic lettering on the marquee, while below, in elegant script, the slogan:

Investigating the dark cubbyholes of otherworldly experience . . .

Uncle C insisted on that *dot-dot-dot* at the end, even though he knew it threw off the marquee's alignment and made the whole thing look a bit sloppy. "The *dot-dot-dot* is key," he told me. "The *dot-dot-dot* means there's so much more, yes? Without the *dot-dot-dot*, how could we invoke"—his hands performed a whimsical arabesque—"the mysteries of infinity?"

The Occultorium was small and cramped, every square foot packed with arcana. Its walls were painted matte black, which gave the sanctum a hazy aspect even in broad daylight. The shelves displayed books with titles like *A Voodoo Doll Spell Book*, *Practical Demonology*, *They Exist!* and *Witch Hunting Made Easy*. The glass-topped display cases held tarot card decks, Ouija boards, build-it-yourself voodoo doll kits, curse amulets, anti-curse amulets, silver skulls, all-seeing eyes, puzzle boxes, dowsing rods, jars of "Nightmare Jam" ("Ingredients: milk, cream, Hendrick's gin, 1 follicle of virgin's hair"), ritual chalices encrusted with gaudy rhinestones, and one-of-a-kind objects with unspeakable backstories.

"So that's *really* a shard of rock from Stonehenge?" a customer might ask.

"Its authenticity is irreproachable," my uncle would intone. "It was smuggled out by an outcast Druid at great peril to his everlasting soul."

To me it looked an awful lot like the schist found in great abundance in the quarry three blocks from Uncle C's house.

A stuffed raven loomed over the cash register. My uncle had glued an unlit cigarette in the crook of its beak, which he felt gave it a suitably "rock 'n' roll" look. Uncle C would stand beneath the raven's spread wingspan, long arms draped on the countertop in mimicry of the bird. Foreboding body language aside, in both dress and demeanour Uncle C did not match his merchandise. He favoured acid-washed jeans and garish tie-dye shirts bought by the dozen from the silkscreen joint two storefronts down.

The shop did poorly. Tourists were keen on T-shirts emblazoned with goofy slogans, saltwater taffy, junk trinkets and fudge. They were less enthused about six-packs of garlic-infused vampire stakes or a copy of *The Necronomicon* signed by famed Satanist Anton Szandor LaVey. They'd wander in with a camera slung around their necks and a streak of zinc oxide down their noses, hoping to find a magic kit or maybe some Mexican jumping beans. Instead they got a shop full of bizarre items presided over by a man who looked like a Grateful Dead roadie.

"Oh," they'd often say while grappling with the shop's strange wares. And then: "*Oh.*"

After which, they'd leave.

If a customer should linger, Uncle C would say, "What is your pleasure, seeker? Look carefully. Something might just"—here he would dab the air in front of his face with the tip of one elongated finger—"call out to you."

He'd cheerfully extol the properties of mandrake root—which is said to scream when pulled from the ground—or lemon verbena, an ingredient in curse sachets that also happened to make a heavenly poultry rub. His sales pitches rarely hit pay dirt. On those rare occasions when someone did the unthinkable and bought something, my uncle would wrap the item with great care, place it in a black Mylar bag and press it to the customer's chest with the words, "Be well, and may your purchase serve you faithfully on your journey." These customers left his shop intoxicated, elated and a bit spooked.

The Occultorium was also overrun with kids in search of drugs. Lexington Galbraith, who owned the neighbouring video emporium, had a sideline as a purveyor of pot to local high-schoolers. The students figured if a video store sold dime bags of skunky pot, the Occultorium must sell some trippy pharmaceuticals. Wormwood LSD, maybe? But while my uncle held a relaxed view on drugs—"Whatever gives you that extrasensory edge, Jake, my boy"—he never sold them.

"You hear about the guy who took too much blotter acid and had a lifelong trip?" he asked me once. "The cops were outside his door, coming to bust him, so he ate his whole stash. Now he thinks he's a glass of orange juice. He's in the nuthatch, bug-eyed and shivering, terrified someone's coming to drink him."

Uncle C cracked a bottle of Yoo-Hoo, took a deep swallow, levelled his eyes on me.

"And *that*, Jake, is why you shouldn't do drugs."

A beat.

"Probably shouldn't."

A red rotary phone sat in the back room of the Occultorium. It had no finger wheel, meaning it couldn't make outgoing calls. Calls could only come in, and they did with regular frequency. Whenever the phone rang, the red light on its casing flashing moodily, my uncle would hustle into the backroom, close the door, pick up the receiver and intone, "The line is secure. You are in safe hands. Now speak."

This phone—he called it the "Bat Phone"—brought spectacular news. Over the years Uncle C had cultivated a network of mystics and paranoiacs and those who saw the world at a different skew. Crackpots who strung eight deadbolts down their doors, drank only deionized water and refused medical X-rays. My father archly referred to them as "Card-carrying members of the Tinfoil-Hat Brigade." The fact of the Bat Phone, and its callers, also gave my father the clearance to refer to the Occultorium as "the Bermuda Triangle, where common sense vanished without a trace." My father could fire off the zingers when it came to Uncle C—and when it came to the store, my mother couldn't argue with him.

The Bat Phone connected my uncle to an underground network called "Those Who Know the TRUTH." Every few days a fresh nugget would filter in over the line.

"No!" Uncle C would say. "Can this be corroborated? Of course, not by the press. They're in cahoots. What about the *Watcher* . . . and Henkel . . . *both* of them?" He'd feverishly scratch notes in a spiral-bound notebook. "Huh. This story might have legs."

One afternoon while my uncle was in the storage room I flipped through his notebook of Bat Phone findings.

- *Blood-chilling accident at Shreveport circus . . . performing dwarf bounces off trampoline and into the mouth of an underfed hippo. Swallowed him like a peanut. Verifiable? Carnie cover-up?*
- *Celebrity tattle: Cher Bono had bottom ribs surgically removed to look more supple.*
- *News from the* Watcher: *Venomous snakes lurk in ball pits at fast-food restaurants . . .*
- *Update from Dark Heshie: El Chupacabra sightings as far north as Jefferson City, Missouri. Questionable veracity: climate wouldn't seem to suit the Mexican demon's poisonous blood. In light of recent items, beginning to think Dark Heshie is NOT a credible source.*

After one of his intel-gathering sessions, my uncle would work the cramp out of his writing hand and say, "Jake, swear to keep this secret?"

I'd nod dutifully, only to have my uncle disclose something quite hideous, such as, "Let's just say that a certain fast-food chain will soon be legally prohibited from using the word 'chicken' in their name. Why? Because, Jake, my boy, they're not frying *chickens* anymore. My sources tell me the chain hired a geneticist to engineer a creature that provides all the benefits of a chicken with none of the waste. No feathers to pluck, no feet, no beak, not even a head to lop off. The geneticist tinkered with the DNA helix and created a GMO: genetically modified organism. Nothing but a big lump of skin, all oversized breasts and juicy drumsticks. Instead of a head there's just a sucking, fluttering pink *hole*."

Drinking in my expression of abject horror, he'd press on, "I know, I know! What kind of a life . . . ? These pitiable creatures are housed in giant warehouses, stacked up in cages like toy blocks, kept alive by intravenous tubes pumping a nutrient-rich slurry." His voice dropped to a gravedigger's whisper. "It's *not* chicken."

While Uncle C would've nursed his beliefs without any outside support, he did have one leery listener other than myself: his neighbouring store-owner, Lexington Galbraith. If a blind, three-legged racehorse named "Next Stop: Glue Factory" were racing down at the Fort Erie track, you can bet Lex Galbraith would've bet his life savings on the nose of that nag. This misguidance was reflected in his appearance: at forty, Lex looked to be pushing sixty. He was short and stooped, with a hangdog expression. The cloud of depression enrobing him was supported by his attire; he favoured black turtlenecks even in summertime, giving him the look of a dour mime.

One thing Lex did have going for him for many years was his thriving video shop. It was the eighties, and home video was king. But, Lex being Lex, he made a crucial miscalculation.

"Betamax is the wave of the future," he told my uncle.

"I don't know, Lex. If it was the best, wouldn't they have called it, *hmm*, Alphamax?"

"Don't be a fool, Cal. It's merely a name. They're smaller than VHS cassettes, with superior sound and sharper definition. A Ferrari to VHS's Yugo."

He changed the name of his shop from Lex's Video Hideaway to So Beta! to reflect his conviction. By the time my twelfth summer rolled around, tumbleweeds were drifting through the aisles of So Beta!

"Beta *is* better. You want to know the problem?" Lex lamented. "People are stupid."

As for my uncle's convictions about global conspiracies and forbidden lore, on the one hand Lex exhibited benevolent tolerance towards those views—"*I guess it's conceivable, Cal, in the sense that almost anything is*"—while on the other hand manifesting total disbelief in them—"*. . . but let me be perfectly clear in saying that I find your theories to be ratbag insane.*"

It gradually struck me that Lex savoured his role as

the skeptical counterbalance. When Uncle C brought up the newest tidbit to come in via the Bat Phone, Lex would cock a Spockian eyebrow. "Open your mouth, Cal."

"Why?"

"I need to check for a bobber. You swallowed that one hook, line, and sinker."

One afternoon early in that summer, I was eavesdropping as Uncle C and Lex discussed possible UFO activity in connection with a spate of crop circles in Kansas. Lex had just stepped out when a boy about my age entered the shop so silently that the bell above the door barely tinkled. He moved down the shelves with a forward hunch, seeking, curious. He wore pegged blue jeans, a plain white T-shirt and a baseball cap.

My uncle said, "Calvin Sharpe at your service. How may I help you?"

The boy glanced up sharply. "Billy Yellowbird," he said. "I'm here because my setsuné just died."

"Nice to meet you, young Master Yellowbird," Uncle C said. "I'm sorry to hear about your grandmother."

It never failed to amaze me, the things my uncle knew—including, apparently, a smattering of what I later learned was Dene.

"My shop specializes in occult items, Billy. I'm not

sure I have what you're seeking. What do you believe you're looking for?"

Billy worked his tongue nervously between his molars, then said: "I wondered if you did one of those things where you talk to dead people."

"A seance? Hmm, well yes, I don't do them myself but I could put you in touch with the right people. Can I ask, isn't there someone you could talk to instead of a spirit medium?"

"They are all up north still. We just moved here."

Uncle C beckoned to Billy. "Come around those shelves so we can talk face to face."

The raven's grand wingspan cast a shadow over Billy's face. My uncle set his elbows on the counter and rested his chin in his cupped palms, gazing at the new boy in town, eye to eye.

"Would you like to dream of your grandmother? Would that help?"

Billy said, "I don't remember my dreams anymore."

"Few of us do," Uncle C said. "But I know a recipe. The elixir of dreams. I can mix it with a few of these items."

He gestured to a shelf holding glass jars stoppered with flat corks the size of saucers. Their contents were inked on faded labels: Toad Flax, Blood Meal, Jacklebeet, Powdered Snakeskin.

"I'll put it in a tea bag," he went on. "At night, put

Craig Davidson

on a kettle and pour boiling water over it. Wait for it to cool, then drink it all. It'll taste ghastly."

Billy said, "And then?"

"If it works—it doesn't always—it will open your dreaming channels. Galvanize your subconscious circuitry and invite your grandmother to make contact. You would dream her into existence again, just for a while, to say a proper goodbye."

Billy patted his pockets. "I'll have to owe you."

"First elixir's on the house. If it works, you may pony up for the next one."

The deal consummated, Uncle C took down jars and doled out ingredients with a tapered spoon tipped with a satyr's horn. He set allotments of powder on a square of parchment, *tsk*ing to himself when he laid down too much, "Butterfingers, Calvin."

Billy and I observed, rapt, until "Blast! I'm out of tea bags. What a cock-up." A light came into my uncle's eyes. "I may have some in the basement . . . hold the phone, back in a trice."

He hustled into the recesses of the shop. I heard the trap door open, then his feet thud on the stairs leading to the basement. Billy and I stood at the counter while my uncle shoved boxes around below us.

We waited in uneasy silence until a sound travelled up the basement steps. To this day, I have a hard time describing it. Kind of a strangled moan.

Had Uncle Calvin hurt himself? Was he having a cardiac episode? My fifth-grade French teacher, Monsieur Levesque, had one near the end of the school year. He'd collapsed in the teachers' lounge and rumour had it his lit cigarette burnt a hole through the little alligator on his Lacoste shirt.

"Uncle C?"

When he didn't answer, I said to Billy, "I'll go check. You can stay up here."

My footsteps echoed on the wooden steps as I went down. The basement was bigger than the shop above, lit by bare bulbs staggered along a low ceiling. The space was packed to the beams with boxes and other items covered in drop cloths. Despite the sepulchral lighting and the cobwebs that hung like silken parachutes in every corner, I'd never found it all that creepy.

"Uncle C?"

"Over here."

He'd shoved a bunch of stuff aside to clear a path into the furthest reaches of the basement. I found him sitting with a packet of tea bags on his lap. He smiled when he saw me but there was something odd about his eyes.

"It's so . . . so very strange, Jake."

I didn't like the flutter in his voice and the aspect in his eyes: as if something was capering, barely visible, in each pupil. A tiny creature moving towards the light while flinching from it at the same time.

"I . . . I forgot all about it."

I followed his pointing finger to the object he'd unearthed during his search. It looked like a battered old suitcase.

"Help me lug it upstairs, will you?"

I don't want to. I couldn't say why—it was nothing more than a boy's innocent intuition—but I wanted nothing to do with that case.

I helped my uncle lug it upstairs. He set it on the counter in front of Billy. He unsnapped the brass clasps and lifted the top. A name was stamped in faded gold foil lettering on the underside of the lid: Psycho-Phone.

"It's called a 'spirit phone,' boys."

What lay inside resembled a portable phonograph player, the type that went out of fashion in the 1920s. It had a complex series of rotating rods, sprockets and brass gears, and a gauge numbered just like the face of a clock but with four hands instead of two, like a diver's chronograph. Sitting in the place where a turntable would normally be was an old See 'N Say toy, the same kind I'd had as a young boy: a red dial that went round and round until it settled on one of the twelve animals circling its perimeter and a voice said, *The cow says moo* or *The cat says meow*.

"It's been modified," said Uncle C, unhooking a

silver horn from the lid and coupling it to the main mechanism. "It was built to record its impressions on wax cylinders, which were what people used before vinyl swept the nation."

"What does it do?" I asked.

"Opens a connection, or so they say."

He unclipped two fittings at the edge of the case, levered the mounting up and withdrew something from underneath. It was another electronic toy—a Speak & Spell—wired to the original components.

"Thomas Edison built the first spirit phone," Uncle C said, "to try to contact his sainted mother."

He unrolled an electrical cord from the base of the Psycho-Phone.

"Would you like to try to contact your grand-mother, Billy?"

"Yes."

"This is an unorthodox method."

Billy said drily, "Looks like it."

"Using a spirit phone is like patching into a party line," my uncle said. "There's a million spirits floating around. It's not for sure that your grandma will break through the static, though I'm sure she'd want to."

Uncle C put his hand on Billy Yellowbird's shoulder—or almost did: his long fingers hovered milli-metres above Billy's T-shirt, not quite touching. He said quietly, "Not all of the dead mean us well. There's evil—I mean genuine, profound evil—mixed in with the good. You never know what you're going to pull in. Maybe something quite awful."

"I'm not scared," Billy said. I was shocked to hear it, as the possibility of a malevolent entity invading a seance curdled the marrow in my own bones.

"What do you want to speak to her about?" I asked.

Billy traced a circle with his fingertip on the countertop.

"We moved here from Slave Lake. My mom, my sister and my setsuné. My mother, she got a job at the hospital. She's a nurse. We have a house on Harvard Street. But my setsuné, she didn't like it. She missed her river, her trees."

"We have a river here," my uncle said. "Trees, too."

"*Her* river, *her* trees. So, she got sick and so . . . she died."

"And you can't take her back, because it's illegal to transport her body beyond town limits," my uncle said.

Billy showed my uncle his palms. "I don't know the reasons why, but we can't bring her home."

Uncle C rolled the plug of the Psycho-Phone between his fingers. It was frayed as if mice had nibbled it. Maybe, I thought, the phone wouldn't work.

"You just want to know that she's made it safely to the other side?"

"That's all."

My uncle nodded. "Then let's see what we can see."

He inserted the plug in the outlet. For a prolonged heartbeat, nothing happened. Then the machine shuddered to life. The phone rattled on the counter, jittering sideways until it nearly toppled off the edge. The Speak & Spell screen glowed blood-red before blipping out. Pinholes of smoke rose up, carrying the smell of charred dust.

"Not to worry," said Uncle C. "It hasn't been used in a long time."

The Psycho-Phone gave off a hum that prickled my skin. The air seemed to warm slightly; I imagined molecules tightening and rubbing together to create a friction I felt in the fillings of my teeth.

"Your grandmother's name," my uncle prodded. "Type it on the keypad."

Billy pressed letters on the Speak & Spell. A-N-N-I-E.

"Now press 'Enter.'"

Billy's thumb dimpled the red square on the keypad—

AaaaNIE.

The word was spat from the plastic speaker in the toy's uncanny voice. The name hung in the air, disharmonious, while the dial on the See 'N Say began to spin.

The duck says . . .

The dial didn't stop the way it was supposed to, the way it always had when I'd played with it as a little boy. It just kept spinning and spinning—

The duck says . . . says . . . says . . .

The decal on the dial—an apple-cheeked farmer with a shovel—was partway peeled off, flapping silently as it spun faster and faster.

Say "quack," I thought desperately. *Just say "quack."*

When the machine didn't oblige, I wrenched my gaze away and looked out the shop window. I needed to see there was still daylight outside—that there still *was* an outside—that the Occultorium hadn't been lifted up like the farmhouse in *The Wizard of Oz*, spinning off into space . . .

Helplessly, my eyes were drawn back to the phone. It was making a new sound, one that didn't emanate from the See 'N Say. It came from the silver horn.

Years later, as a medical resident, I'd listen to a recording from inside a human skull. All is quiet inside our heads, but by amplifying the natural magnetic impulses it's possible to hear the living clockwork of a brain. This particular brain belonged to a patient with a late-stage tumour anchored in her occipital lobe. The recording lasted a minute or so. Its only constant was an unearthly hiss that crested and ebbed in time with the patient's blood flow. It sounded like waves of static crashing on a distant beachhead. Within those waves, or outside them, were other noises: pings and crackles and purrs, liquid gurgles, a sound like the pitter-patter of feet dancing on a rain-rinsed tin roof. The professor told us they were made by magnetic waves bending around the rim of the patient's brain. But he couldn't tell us if we were hearing the patient's thoughts themselves, or perhaps the sounds of the tumour creeping through her mind.

Sitting in that classroom listening to a stranger's brain, I thought back to that afternoon in the Occultorium. At first, the sounds the spirit phone made were almost one with the run-of-the-mill noises of the shop: the tick of the clock and creak of the old floorboards. Almost but not *quite*, as if whatever was making them wanted us to know it was being sly. Toying with us. The phone's sprockets and cogs wound as the sounds took on shape and weight. It was as if somebody was twisting the tuner knob on a radio without stopping long enough to find a station, pulling in signals from beyond the reach of spacecraft or satellite, beyond the last collapsing star. . . .

I looked at Uncle Calvin. The black pinholes of his irises glittered as they had in the basement.

Now, noise pulsed from the phone: throbs and burrs, something like Morse code followed by a vibrating wire that quilled the hairs of my inner ear. The old circuitry was struggling to transmute the transmissions it was receiving into sounds the silver horn could relay. I got the sense that the phone was the wrong machine for the job, that what we were trying to do was no different from trying to tell the time of day using a thermometer. The dial on the See 'N Say spun and spun and spun. . . . I heard things. Screams in a dense sonic mist, wind sawing across rusted metal, something bubbling, rainfall like ten-penny nails. I would have slammed the lid of the Psycho-Phone, crumpling the horn between the lips of the case, but I couldn't move, was para-lyzed, the sounds ebbing into whale-songs as some-thing else built behind them—a sinister presence running behind those melancholy arias. Soon all I could hear was horrid stifled breathing, breaths built out of whispers, realizing too late that the cadence of those breaths matched the rapid beat of my own heart.

Something's coming, I thought. *Something horrible.*

Within moments, the phone would give birth to a voice. I was positive of it. And when it spoke, that voice would not be human, or belong to anything that ever had been—

The noises cut out.

My uncle was on his knees with the plug in his

hands. I was terrorized by the prospect that those sounds might persist despite the power cut, but the phone stayed mercifully dead.

"That was"—my uncle laughed, *hah-ho!*—"a little intense, wasn't it?"

Billy's face remained serene, but his fingertips were bloodless white where they gripped the countertop. He saw me looking and stuffed his hands in his pockets.

"Atmospheric harmonics," my uncle assured us. "The vacuum tubes probably tuned in a distorted feed of CHSC AM radio. Nothing more than harmless signals."

I wiped the clammy sweat from my forehead. "Signals," I said robotically.

Uncle C shut the case. "Billy, this is a delicate question but—your grandmother, has she been, well, has she been laid to rest officially yet?"

Billy said, "No, but we already took her to the . . . the . . ."

"Undertaker?" I said.

"Yes, him. I didn't like him."

Cataract City's undertaker was named Stanley Rowe. He was tall, discreet, suitably funereal, with a vinegary scent wafting off his clothes—a smell I now know to be formaldehyde.

"Undertakers can be a shady bunch," Uncle C agreed. "One of their common scams is to sell their customers' loved ones to medical supply companies to turn into skeletons—you know, the ones that hang in anatomy classrooms. They fill the coffin with sandbags and into the ground it goes, and nobody ever the wiser."

"I don't think Mr. Rowe does that." I couldn't say why, in that moment, I felt the need to stick up for the professional integrity of a man I hardly knew, but this seemed to mollify my uncle.

"Jake's right, Stanley's not one of those bad eggs. Listen, what would you like us to do?" he asked Billy simply. I noted that he was involving me in whatever this was—but I had nothing better to do, and besides, I wanted to help Billy too.

"I just want to know Setsuné is safe and happy, wherever she is."

"There's only one way to assure you of that," my uncle said.

We made a plan and parted company soon afterwards. That night, tucked in bed, I would replay the sight of my uncle's eyes shining strangely—and years later, looking at things forensically, as surgeons do, I realized that was the start of everything to follow. What had been buried had taken root again. In the basement under my uncle's shop, where he stumbled upon a device whose provenance he could no longer recall.

iv.

We broke into the funeral home at eight o'clock the following night.

Uncle C, Billy and I met a few blocks up the road, near the cemetery gates. By the time I pedalled up on my BMX the sky had gone ashy above the treetops. Billy was there already. We waited in what felt like companionable silence, leaning on our handlebars, until Uncle C rode up on his ten-speed. My uncle didn't own a car. I'd never seen him behind the wheel, not once in my life.

"All right, boys, sure you want to go through with this? No shame in second thoughts."

Billy nodded. After a moment I did, too. I understood instinctively that Uncle C had invited me along in hopes I'd find a new friend. But the invite came with a catch. To gain Billy's friendship, I'd have to see a dead body.

Uncle C shouldered his satchel and said, "Onward, soldiers."

We approached the funeral home through the cemetery. Tombstones cast shadows on the sun-scalded grass behind the cast-iron fence. A raven—smaller than the one in the Occultorium, but big enough— observed us from its perch atop the granite mausoleum crypt, moonlight reflecting off its black doll's eyes.

The Rowe Funeral Home stood on a hill that backed onto the cemetery. Its trio of greenish copper rooftops—covering what I would soon discover to be the parlour itself, the coffin showroom and the embalming chamber—loomed behind a network of spidery tree branches. A single light burnt in the cemetery beyond, its glow shimmering across the earth like a flame racing up a fuse. I wondered if it could be the lamp of a watchman, held aloft as he patrolled this brooding boneyard.

"It looks scarier than it really is," my uncle assured us.

We headed up the gravelled drive. The sly sounds of night infiltrated my ears: the rustlings of unseen bodies in the grass or hunching behind the mossy tombstones. I drew closer to my uncle, reaching for his hand . . . then stopped myself from grabbing it, but it was a near thing.

Our moon-washed expressions peered back at us from the darkened windows of the building. Uncle C led us to a door set in a brick alcove.

"This is the embalming room," he whispered. "Behind this door is, well, death. Sanitary and sterilized, but still death."

He produced a kit from his satchel. Inside were tools that looked like those the dentist used to pick at teeth. He selected one and fit it into the door's lock. Next, he cocked his head, frowned and, in a manner that made the movement seem like an afterthought, turned the knob.

"Will you look at that. My skills of skulduggery will not be required." He crouched before us. "Billy, your grandmother is behind here. Are you ready for that?"

Billy inhaled, held the breath and nodded.

"And you, Jake? You can always wait out here."

The prospect of waiting alone in that alcove struck me as worse than whatever lay behind the door. "I'll come."

Uncle C produced a flashlight and waved us on. We trailed him inside, following the cone of light. A smell hit my nostrils: bitter and pruney, like the air wafting out of a jar of ancient preserves. The hallway funnelled into a high-ceilinged chamber. My uncle's flashlight shone on washtubs and glass canisters of gauze and cloth bandages. The room was dominated by a stainless-steel table. A shape rested upon it, covered in a sheet.

Something clutched at my elbow. I almost screamed, but realized just in time that it was Billy who'd grabbed me. His eyes shone white as high beams in a flashlight's glow. He let go of my arm guiltily.

"Sorry. I . . . thought I saw it move."

I wished Billy hadn't said that. Now all I could think about was the shape sitting up, the sheet falling away and a gleaming skull pinning me with a baleful glare as its wrinkled-apricot eyes rolled around in its sockets—

"It's perfectly safe, boys. We're the only lively things in here." My uncle shone the light on the wall, which was inset with vaults. Their polished doors and handles reminded me of filing cabinets—which they were. Human filing cabinets.

My uncle said, "Your grandmother is in this one here."

"How do you know?" Billy said.

"A little birdy told me." He wrapped his fingers around the handle. "Ready?"

Billy said, "Yes."

The trolley rolled out with a velvety rumble, its rails lined with ball bearings. As the cool air inside the vault mixed with the warmer air of the room, plumes of mist bloomed up. The mist shredded away to reveal a body laid out on the steel, shrunken in the way only death can shrink a person. Small and stiff and . . .

A man. Obviously and unmistakably a man.

"This . . . *hmm*," said Uncle C. "This fellow isn't your grandma, is he?"

"No," Billy confirmed. "She looks different than him."

The man's lips were papery worms. His teeth were grey as gravestones and had little cracks in them like the hairline fractures in granite. Uncle C touched the tips of his fingers to the man's forehead.

"Humblest apologies, good sir. Back to your rest."

He shut the vault. "Sorry, boys. My fault entirely."

Billy and I looked at one another. Billy's eyebrow went up just a bit: *This uncle of yours—is he for real?*

"I know where she must be," my uncle said.

He opened a door leading down another hall. The flashlight's glow bobbed along walls clad in wallpaper the colour of crushed mulberries. We entered the casket showroom. Our shoes kicked up blue sparks on the carpet. Coffins were propped up on catafalques. My uncle strode around the showroom with his gangling lope, searching. In the uncertain light, he looked like a skeleton jingly-jangling through the catacombs. He collided with a jumble of metal wreath stands and said, "Blast it all!" softly.

Billy had stopped at a coffin that glowed like a giant lozenge. The "Celestial Sleeper," sticker price $990. His fingers walked up the wood and along the silk cushioning.

"Big," he whispered. "Softer than my bed."

Uncle C said, "Over here."

He'd located another room holding a single casket.

It was so cold inside that our breath came out in misty vapours.

"This is the staging room," he told us. "It's where the body waits, all made up, for the first showing in the morning."

He laid his palms on the casket lid. "She's in here, Billy, I promise you."

"Show me," Billy said. My uncle lifted the lid.

The woman inside looked like Billy's grandmother. Same skin colour as her grandson—only paler now, as was natural—same elegant forehead and nose. Her head was propped on a satin pillow, arms crossed over her chest. Her eyes were closed and her face serene. I remember hoping all faces settled into such expressions once the life had flowed out of them.

Billy touched his grandma's cheek as if to make sure she was really there. He pulled back with a slight sigh, then spoke a few words I couldn't understand.

"We can close it now," he said.

My uncle led us back out through the showroom. Our eyes had adjusted and we moved sure-footedly amongst the coffins—until I spotted something unexpected and stifled a scream.

A figure stood in the corner, so still that at first I'd mistaken the shape for another casket. I came to a dead stop facing it. The vein in my throat ticked a nervous rhythm as a face swam out of the murk. The undertaker, Stanley Rowe. He stood watching us without anger, unmoving, silent as a sentinel.

"Hustle up," my uncle said, spiriting me out of the room.

I glanced over my shoulder to warn Uncle C about Mr. Rowe . . . and saw something. It was one of those moments when the world doesn't make sense, but later, when you see events in their proper light, understanding sinks in.

My uncle was looking straight at Mr. Rowe. Their eyes met across the dark air and my uncle . . . he *nodded*. The slightest tip of his chin.

Outside, the night air chilled the sweat between my shoulder blades. We moved from the shadow of the funeral home, through the trees into the graveyard. The moon glossed each blade of grass in a wrap of silver. We walked, letting the adrenalin seep out of our pores, until we came upon a freshly dug gravesite.

My uncle sat with his legs dangling into the open grave. He gestured for us to do the same. We each claimed one side of the rectangular hole. The headstone sat in the final side, with no name yet on it. The stonemason would come by to engrave it tomorrow.

"This is where she's going," Billy said with sorrowful certainty.

The rumble of the falls carried up from the Niagara River basin, rolling along the streets and barren parkland.

"Will she be able to hear the river she missed, down there under the ground?" Billy asked my uncle. "How will she see the trees—her trees from back home?"

"What I hope you understand, Billy, is that the only thing going into this hole is your grandmother's body. And our bodies themselves?" My uncle tweezed the skin of his arm and let go. "Just vessels to bear us along. The guiding part of her, the part you loved and that loved you . . . it's already gone. It's part of the atmosphere now, like the steam rising off a bath. So yes, she can see those trees. She can see the monkeys in the Brazilian rainforest or the rocks on the moon if she wants."

"Or the river that flows into Slave Lake," Billy said.

"Of course, yes. All that's left now is the ceremony. Doesn't really matter if she's in a coffin or a canoe or a fire. The ceremony is about respect for the dead and a sense of ending for the living. Every story needs its conclusion, yes?"

"Thank you," Billy said.

Uncle C looked relieved. "You're most welcome."

"Thank you for coming," Billy said to me.

"Oh." Surprised, I grinned. "Yeah, sure. I liked it."

"Sorry about grabbing your arm."

I waved it off. "I mean, it *was* creepy."

"I can't fathom why," my uncle said, genuinely mystified. "Death and life are just different sides of the same natural state."

Billy said, "Uh, no, it was really creepy."

He and I laughed—the first time we'd done that together.

Uncle C pulled a shoebox out of his satchel and set it on his lap. The box was tied in butcher's twine knotted into a bow. "More than a century ago, there lived a man named Charles Fort. His name will be unfamiliar to you. His ideas are not taught in schools. He died a penniless pariah, as has many a great man. Fort believed in a place up there." My uncle crooked a finger skyward. "Not heaven. Closer than the planets, even closer than the moon, but un-glimpsed. He called this place the Super-Sargasso Sea. The Sea of Lost Things."

My uncle's fingers fussed with the bow, but he did not untie the box, not yet.

"Fort recorded his findings in *The Book of the Damned*. In his eyes, that was us. Humans were the damned for failing to see what was right in front of us. He hypothesized that up there, ten miles above, you will encounter a gelatinous membrane—how else would the stars twinkle, if not for their light quivering through gelatin?" He chuckled. "Well, this was before the space race. Fort believed the Lost Sea hovered beyond that layer, that there were invisible worlds in the sky. Some took the shape of spokes or wheels, others were giant sentient beings. Fort reported seeing a vast dark thing like a crow of unholy dimensions poised over the moon."

Billy sat with his hands braced on his knees, leaning towards my uncle's hypnotic voice—I worried that if he leaned any further, he'd topple into the grave.

"Fort theorized that things from our world were drawn into this Lost Sea—sucked up, as if with a giant vacuum—only to fall back to earth, horridly altered. Falls of fish, dead and stiff. When those fish were fried in a pan, they turned into hissing blood. Black snowflakes, too, which Fort claimed to be the burn-off of alien factories forever churning between the stars. Rains the colour of India ink, of caterpillars, of ants the size of wasps and of spiders' webs. Fort recounts an occurrence in northern Quebec where an inland lake was found covered in clumps of hair like floating toupées."

"Why would aliens drop hair on us?" I said.

"That, Fort did not care to elaborate on." My uncle patted the box. "Now, I found this downstairs the other day during my hunt for those pesky tea bags."

He untied the twine and lifted the lid. Billy and

I stared into the box, its contents arrayed under the moonlight.

"They're called fairy crosses."

Inside the shoebox sat a pair of crude crucifixes. Instead of wood or stone, they were made out of white crystal, like the sparkling formations inside a geode.

"According to Fort, a tiny race the size of fairies descended from the Lost Sea. Their spacecraft were never discovered, but why would they be? No bigger than a can of corn, I'm sure. When these explorers died, their kin buried them in matchbox coffins. Over time their bodies atomized, flowed up through the ground like spring buds, and emerged as these."

"Those are aliens' bodies?" said Billy, wonderstruck.

"Only what's left. No life, only the residual beauty. Put your hands out."

Uncle C set one cross in each of our hands.

"I thought we could leave them here. They've been cooped up inside this box for too long. What do you say, Billy?"

After a brief deliberation, Billy positioned his cross in front of the gravestone. He looked at me encouragingly, so I did the same.

"Ah," said Uncle C, "this is a suitable spot indeed."

He settled the lid on the box and tucked it back into the satchel.

"We could have more fun like this, fellas. There

are places I know, places in our city, where the barriers between our world and the spirit realm are full of holes. Things go slip-sliding through all the time."

"Scary things?" I said.

"Nothing we can't handle, Jake. And you'd have a knowledgeable guide. You know I'd never put you in danger, don't you?"

I caught an unfamiliar thread of desperation in Uncle C's voice, as if he wanted me to nod, which is what I did.

"So, what do you boys say—make it a weekly thing. The Saturday Night Ghost Club."

Looking back, I am struck by how precious little it takes to convince an unwilling outsider and the new kid in town to agree to any plan, even one that involved following a gangly middle-aged man into haunted territories.

"Ho-ho, then we have a pact."

My uncle spanked his hands, then glanced at his watch. "We ought to toddle off . . . and let's keep what happened tonight between us, hmm?"

V.

I returned home to find my father drinking a beer at the kitchen table. He was still dressed in his work clothes with his tie looped around his neck like a garrotte. He'd been coming home late most of that spring. The GM plant was cutting back. Everyone was crabbing about the Japanese, but my father conceded they made better cars. For the first time ever, Dad was issuing foreclosure papers. Houses, small businesses. He'd been forced to lower the boom on his own friends and neighbours.

"Where you been?"

"Uncle C's shop."

"Big news come in over the Bat Phone? Leprechauns massing forces under the falls, planning a sneak attack to recover their stolen gold?"

"Come on, Dad."

He gave an arch nod at the clock. "Your uncle keeping extra-late hours?"

Lying to my father was risky—he had a bloodhound's way of sniffing out deceptions—but Uncle C had sworn me to secrecy. I opted for diversionary tactics.

"There was this new kid, Billy."

Dad's eyebrow tilted up. "A buddy?"

"I don't know about that."

"It's hard to meet new people, Jake, and I know

65

your"—my father puffed his cheeks up and blew out between pursed lips—"*interests* aren't always the same as other boys'. Which is absolutely fine. But if this Billy shares some interests, could be the start of a beautiful friendship."

I blew at a hair that had fallen over my eye and dropped my voice in mimicry. "Could be the start of a beautiful friendship."

"Ah, screw it. I stole that line from somewhere."

I sat at the table. My father gripped my wrist and turned my fingers up to the light. Too late, I noticed the rime of grave-dirt under my fingernails.

"I know your uncle doesn't keep the world's cleanest shop, but is it *that* dirty?" Dad got up and went to the fridge. "Want a soda?"

I ran a self-conscious hand over the bulge of my stomach. "Mom doesn't like me drinking pop."

"You'll burn it off in this heat." My father dug a grape soda out of the icebox, and another beer for himself. He set my can on the table and popped the tab with one squared-off finger. Then he braced his bottle's cap against the table's edge and slapped his free hand down on his wrist to pop the cap off. He lifted the bottle to his lips, corralled the foam, and sat with his legs stretched out in a V, toes up, one arm slung over the seatback. A lot of grown men in my hometown sat like that.

"Light beer. All your mom lets me drink anymore. Only two a night, too." He stewed on this for a moment before brightening. "It's best for all concerned."

He regarded me evenly. His oft-broken nose hooked to the left. I suppose he found it weird that he'd ended up with a son like me: spacey and bookish, scared of every little thing. I wondered what kind of boy he'd expected.

"Your uncle . . ."

"Yeah?"

"*Yes*, Jake. *Yeah* is for truckers and toll-booth workers. Which are honourable ways to earn a living, but."

I sipped my soda. "Yes?"

"Your uncle Cal is a good man, and he's been through a lot. Your mom and me think it's great, you spending time with him. But . . . when I was a kid I used to wish Peter Pan would show up at my window. He'd spirit me away to the land of make-believe where I could play all day and never grow up."

He rubbed his palm over his squished nose. I sensed he was struggling with what to say, or the right way to say it. "That's a great thing to believe as a boy. Enjoy it now, Jake, my fine feathered friend, because there's nothing quite so odd as seeing Peter Pan all grown up."

"Okay, Dad," I said dutifully, because that's what kids said when adults got weird.

He drew me into a rough hug. Stubble grated my cheek. He smelled of Old Spice and faintly, pleasantly, of malt.

"Up to bed, you strange and beautiful organism."

I left him staring out the kitchen window, waiting for Peter Pan to arrive.

3.

THE SCREAMING TUNNEL

Neurosurgeons constantly grapple with the ways in which the brain can turn feral and lash out at its owner. Which is to say, we must become acquainted with heartbreak.

The girl was eight years old when her file landed on my desk. Earlier that year, her parents noticed that she would drift off in the middle of some task, even those she showed great fondness for such as painting. Her teachers remarked that she had developed the habit of settling her head on her desk and falling fast asleep. In every other respect, she was an active girl. Her energy was good when awake. She simply slept too much.

A week before the operation, the girl's mother noticed her left eye protruding from its socket, as if something was pushing it out. An MRI revealed a mass lodged near her pineal gland. A malignant rhabdoid tumour, an aggressive form of cancer manifesting in children.

She was booked into surgery immediately. My sucker wand transited the lobes of her brain, moving through sticky webs of glia—brain glue, as it is known in our racket—to arrive at the tumour, which lay anchored to her ocular nerve. The delicate procedure was like vacuuming caramelized sugar off a strand of cooked spaghetti. The slightest misstep would snap the nerve and rob the girl of sight in that eye. I removed as much as felt safe before retreating.

The girl and her parents were given a room at the Ronald McDonald House and became fixtures in the hospital halls. Soon, it became clear that the tumour was winning. It was reprogramming the girl's cells. This is why cancer is so aggressive in children: their bodies are growing, and the disease marshals those growth factors for its own ill designs.

The tumour crept out of the girl's ocular vault to infest her brain like the dark legs of a spider protruding from its hidey-hole, severing connections and rewriting memory encodings. Unable to stay awake, the girl took up new residence in a dream-realm. When lucid, she would talk about it—a world she named Jupita. The light there held an unearthly brightness, and rivers flowed the colour of gold. She spoke of glittering cities on the plains where castles towered behind alabaster walls. The girl wandered Jupita's landscape with two companions: a robot, Gunther, and her best friend, a druid named Camphor. They had many thrilling adventures.

The girl slept twenty-three hours a day. She thinned drastically and had to be fed by IV. I asked the unit social worker to keep close watch over her parents. Hard enough to see your child suffer, harder still to have her locked away in the chambers of her own corroding mind. As a surgeon, ostensibly impartial, I didn't know how I felt. I understood their sorrow but also sensed the girl was happy right where she was, in that world of her own summoning.

One afternoon near the end, she awoke and asked for her paint kit. Her mother arranged oils and paper on the bed, but by then the girl didn't recognize her parents. Her mother could have been a nurse, the janitor or any other helpful stranger. Over the next half-hour, she completed two paintings. When they were finished, she slept again. I saw those paintings the next day.

The first was of the robot, Gunther. The second depicted the druid, Camphor. Her constant companions and protectors. Anyone could have spotted the resemblance.

The robot was the spitting image of her father. Camphor bore the face of her mother.

i.

A week after his grandmother's funeral, Billy Yellowbird showed up at the Occultorium with his sister, Dove. She was the girl who had chucked a rock at Percy Elkins.

Until then, I'd taken little notice of the differences between boys and girls. Both were part of that big fleshy blob called *people*, or *humanity*, to use the ten-cent word I'd heard in social studies class. I could say that girls usually had longer hair and smelled nicer than boys (some girls at school had recently discovered Lou Lou perfume, which gave them the scent of vanilla wafers) but until Dove I'd never felt the giddy fizz of electricity that burst from my chest to form a blue-white nimbus in the air of my uncle's shop—a phenomenon I prayed that I alone could see.

Dove eyed the raven above the cash register. "Morbid much?"

Billy hung his head. "Aww, Dove . . ."

She had walked in with the grand strut of a long-legged shore bird. Like Billy, her hair was dark: it shone like a curved mirror in the sunlight falling through the window. Now she strode to the counter, stuck her hand out at my uncle and said, "Hello, hello, hello. My name's Dove, Dove Yellowbird. And that's my brother, Billy."

"They know me," said Billy. "I brought you here, remember?"

"How am I supposed to know who knows you?" To my uncle: "I have to introduce him to everyone. He needs an official greeter half the time."

My uncle gripped Dove's hand in both of his and pumped vigorously. "Dove, an immense pleasure. My name's Calvin. This is my nephew Jake."

When Dove turned to me, my heart made a funny hop behind my rib cage.

"Hey you," she said, either not recognizing me or choosing not to bring up our shared history. "I've heard about you. Billy says you're a good egg."

"*Awww*," Billy moaned.

My uncle laughed. "Good egg. That is an apt descriptor."

A coin of light danced in each of Dove's eyes. They

made me think of sparklers sputtering at the bottom of dark pools.

"Dove Yellowbird," my uncle mused. "A name with two birds."

"Yeah, except doves are symbols of peace and I'm not so peaceful."

Dove was fourteen, two years older than Billy and me, but she seemed a decade older. A tin of Cherry Skol was parked in the front pocket of her jean jacket, a little hockey puck pressed to the denim.

"Cool store, Calvin. Where did you get this stuff?"

"It comes from all over, Dove. This charm amulet here?" He rapped his knuckles on the display glass. "From Egypt. And this monkey's paw? Morocco. This All-Seeing Eye? Romania."

Dove tapped the side of her nose. "And if they happened to have come from a warehouse in Taiwan I guess the tourists wouldn't know the diff, huh?"

"Between you, me and the doorknob?" my uncle said. "No, they wouldn't. You don't believe in much of this, I take it?"

"Much of what?"

My uncle lifted his hand to his ear and spun it lazily at the wrist, a gesture that took in his shop and, quite possibly, the cosmos. "The spirit realm. The paranormal."

"People can believe what they want," Dove said.

"It's great to believe in something. But this guy"—she hooked her thumb at Billy—"believes in anything. Vampires and phantoms and elbow-witches, probably knee- and nose- and butthole- and every other kind of witch, too."

"I thought you said it was okay to believe in something," my uncle said.

"I do," Dove said. "Something, not *everything*."

With that, she turned to leave. Surprising myself, I said, "Where are you going?"

"I don't know, bud. Just out."

"You should all go," my uncle said. "A beautiful day. Why waste it inside?"

Uncle C slipped around the counter to usher us out of the shop. Politely but firmly, he put his palm between my shoulder blades. The Bat Phone rang. He rushed his goodbyes to answer it, leaving the three of us on the sidewalk, where we found Lex Galbraith lounging outside So Beta! smoking a cigarette.

"Please don't think Cal's being impolite," he said. "But when that phone rings, the earth stops. Or starts rotating backwards on its axis. Or is about to collapse from the sand-worm infestation seething under its crust." Lex flapped his arms. "Lord have mercy, the Bat Phone's ringing. Everybody stop everything and answer the *Baaaaat Phone*, or else the Lobstermen of Gamma Seven will enslave the human race."

Lex pinched the heater off his cigarette, stashed the remaining half in the pocket of his turtleneck, nodded to us courteously and went back into So Beta!

"Is that guy always such a weirdo?" Dove said.

"Who, my uncle?" I said.

"Him too," said Dove, "but I meant Turtleneck McGee there."

"I never knew turtlenecks had pockets," Billy remarked.

"Good ones don't," said Dove. "Check that. There's no such thing as a good turtleneck."

ii.

Clifton Hill swarmed with tourists. They infested the sidewalks and clogged up the shopfronts: a sunburnt, tube-socked, sun-visored horde.

We slalomed between the stalks of their pudgy legs. The smell of fried dough and caramel mingled with the coconut sweetness of Hawaiian Tropic suntan oil. Dove flipped out her tobacco puck and packed a pinch of Skol between her lip and gum. I found the fact that she dipped tobacco simultaneously gross and wonderful.

We passed Frankenstein's House of Horrors and

the Criminals' Hall of Fame, where Dove paused to ape the sneer of the waxen Al Capone beside the ticket booth. We elbowed our way up to the viewing rail of the falls. Water tumbled over the lip in a blue sheet, booming into the basin to send up white curtains of mist.

We walked west. I spotted Percy Elkins and one of the Vreeland children, not Terry, kicking the token machine in the arcade at the bottom of Clifton Hill. He didn't see us. A rainbow hovered over the head of the falls. It seemed to keep time with us, dogging our heels until we outdistanced it. Dove spat a stream of tobacco-juice into the gutter, pigeon-necking so it would fly even further. She wiped spittle off her chin.

"Still getting the hang of it."

We rounded into a subdivision. The houses were attached one to the other to the other—they looked like boxcars with windows, all painted the same powder blue. Billy walked up to number 57, unlatched the gate leading into the yard and said, "Well, see ya."

I stood stunned. "Yeah. Uh, bye."

Dove set her hands on her hips. "Are you two kidding me? Billy, you don't have a single friend in town. Kirk Garrow and Rudy Kitto aren't showing up anytime soon, you know. What about you, Jake—got any friends?"

I squinted up at the sky and lied. "Uhh, I mean, a few."

"Come in," she said to me. "Have a glass of Kool-Aid."

The Kool-Aid was cherry-flavoured. Dove poured it from a plastic jug into jelly jars. The kitchen was neat and clean, with moving boxes stacked in the corners.

We went out to the backyard, which was hemmed by a low chain-link fence. I could see all the way down the block, into every yard, with their vegetable patches and teeter-totters and frayed lawn furniture. The Yellowbirds' yard was empty except for a Mister Turtle pool covered with a sheet of plywood.

"Might as well feed the moneymakers," said Dove.

Billy and I trailed her over to the pool, where she shoved the plywood aside and spread her arms in a "voila" gesture.

There, under a few inches of algae-bloomed water, things moved. Torsional shapes, some flicking as if in reaction to the wash of sunlight, others resting perfectly still.

"Are those . . . ?"

"Salamanders," Billy told me.

"Correction, they are black gold," said Dove. "Well, most but not all of them are black. I don't want to generalize."

It was hard to tell how many there were, as Dove

had added a few plate-sized lily pads to the pool. Bulge-eyed salamander heads poked from the frilled rims of the succulents.

"I found two of them down along the river doing their mating dance," Dove said. "And I said to myself, *Hey, here's a buck waiting to be made.*"

"You must really like salamanders," I said.

"These four-legged snot-logs? Take 'em or leave 'em. What I like's money, and that pet shop up the hill, what's its name?"

I said, "Pick of the Critter?"

"Right, those geniuses. They're giving me ten bucks a pop. So far I've got"—squinting into the pool for a head count—"twelve, thirteen, fourteen, and more on the way."

She directed my attention to the translucent sacs clustered like bunches of grapes at the sides of the pool. They had the consistency of bath beads, and I saw flagellate shapes squirming inside some of them.

Dove raised her arms above her head and did a dance on the sun-baked grass. "*Money, money, money, money, moneeee-EEE-eee . . .*"

It was the theme song for the Million Dollar Man—the most treacherous heel and greatest scourge in the entire WWF stable at that time.

"Everyone's got a price, and everyone's gonna pay," she growled, "because the Million Dollar Woman *always* gets her way." She followed up with a praiseworthy rich-millionaire's laugh: *"Ah-ah-HAH-HAH-HA—"*

"You aiming to wake the dead, child?"

Turning at the sound of the unfamiliar voice, I set eyes on the most compressed human being I'd ever seen: compact, with delicate but foreshortened limbs.

"Did I wake you, Mamma?"

The only thing out of place on Mrs. Yellowbird was her hair, which stuck up in sleep-tousled sprigs. "You woke half the neighbourhood. You know I'm on nights this week."

Dove slunk across the grass and sidled up to her mother.

"I'm sorry." She spoke in a breathy baby voice: *Eye sowwee.* She rucked her head under her mother's armpit until Mrs. Yellowbird lifted her arm reluctantly, then snuggled in close.

"Eye sowwee, Mah-mee."

"You feeling okay, Dove?"

Mrs. Yellowbird's voice was light but forced. Dove, who acted like she hadn't heard, kept nuzzling into her mother. Mrs. Yellowbird looked at Billy—something molecular passing between their eyes—before tightening her arm around her daughter's shoulder.

"Dove, baby, did you take your . . ."

Dove's body went stiff. Her eyes flicked anxiously in my direction as though for the first time registering me as a person.

"Thank you for the reminder, Mamma. I'll do so directly."

Dove turned robotically and walked inside the house. The limber sway of her limbs had vaporized: she moved like a person whose joints were wired to servos. Mrs. Yellowbird watched her go, then said to Billy, "Want some lunch?"

"Sure, Mom."

Mrs. Yellowbird followed Dove into the house. I noticed that she walked with a limp. She spun on her heel at the doorway.

"Hey, you," she said. "Who are you?"

"I'm Jake."

"You a friend of Billy's?"

"Maybe."

Mrs. Yellowbird's laugh sounded too robust for her frame. "I got bologna. You'll eat a bologna sandwich?" Before I could answer, she said, "You strike me as a fellow who'll eat just about anything. Hustle up, wash your hands."

I followed Billy down the hall to the bathroom. The door was open, faucet running. Over Billy's shoulder, Dove stood at the sink. Her hair was wet as if she'd dunked her head under the tap. A little orange bottle sat on the sink ledge. Dove stared fixedly into the mirror, the water pattering off the ends of her hair.

Billy shut the door. "There's another bathroom upstairs."

iii.

After lunch, Billy and I spent the afternoon touring my favourite spots. I took him to the condemned dog track, where we raced each other around the red dirt oval on our bikes. Billy beat me easily. I showed him the secret path behind Land of Oceans that led to a pen where the sick animals were quarantined. We saw a deer with a growth the size of a summer squash tethered to its head. The growth bounced against the deer's skull like a Nerf ball.

As an apology for taking him to such a depressing spot, I used the buck-fifty I'd earned mowing my neighbour's lawn to buy candy at the Avondale. A box of Mighty Gobstoppers, a box of Hot N Cool Nerds, red licorice tape, two El Bronco grape-flavoured gum cigars and Gold Rush gum, which came in a cloth sack with a drawstring. We took the haul to a skinny strip of land that jutted into the Niagara River a kilometre upstream of the falls. I used to be scared it would break off like a chunk of ice and carry me over the cataract, but that was half the attraction. It was a risk, taking Billy there. If he went the way of Percy Elkins and every other new kid in town, I'd have to find a new spot soon.

I spilled the contents of the paper bag onto a picnic table some enterprising soul had hauled to the end of the spit. Billy avoided looking at the haul, instead training his eyes on the water where it sucked at the edges of the land like a toothless mouth.

"Want some?" I said.

"It's yours, you bought it."

He couldn't think that I'd invited him out there to watch me eat candy all by myself? I picked up the box of Gobstoppers, tore the cardboard along the perforation and shook a red one out. I rolled it off my palm into his.

"I owe you, Jake," he said.

"It's okay."

"*No*, I owe you."

"Okay."

Billy had never eaten Nerds. I let him have the box and kept the Gobstoppers. We stuck our tongues out to inspect their shifting coloration: blue and red and gangrenous green. We halved the sack of Gold Rush gum, lined the nuggets up on the nicked wood, then chewed them with steely deliberation. We stuck the gum cigars in our pockets for later, and lay back, side by side, on the table while the sugar lit up our nervous systems like pinball machines.

"I heard about him, you know," said Billy.

"About who?"

"Charles Fort. Your uncle said we wouldn't know who he was, but I checked his book out at the library last year. It was called *The Book of the Damned*. Read lots of other books, too."

"About what?"

"Strange happenings, stuff like that. Did you hear about the Philadelphia Experiment?" When I told him no, Billy said, "In World War Two, the government tried to cloak battleships to make them invisible. Scientists used electricity and magnets to bend the light around a ship, right? If you bend it the right way, you can trick the human eye. They used Tesla coils, which are machines to build up a ton of electricity, and Helmholtz coils, these big magnets. They tested the cloaking device on a battleship, the USS *Eldridge*. But something happened."

I sat up. "What?"

"The battleship disappeared for thirty seconds. Vanished off radar, right? Then it showed up again, three hundred miles from where it had been. They found it off the coast of Montauk in Long Island.

Some soldiers went out to it—the ship was floating in a weird green mist—but before their boats reached the battleship they heard the screams."

Billy paused his story to blow a gum-bubble. When it popped, he said: "What they found was, uh, the crewmen all stuck in the ship."

"You mean trapped?"

"Yeah, but not like how you think. Stuck *in* the ship. Their bodies were . . . I don't know the word. It was like"—spreading the fingers on each hand, Billy linked them together and squeezed—"into the metal, you see?"

"You mean welded?"

"Sure, welded," he said, putting his hands back by his sides and closing his eyes. "They were part of the ship. Stuck in doors and walls, their head and shoulders on one side and their chest and legs on the other. A lot of them were dead but some were still alive. Others weren't there at all. Out of the fifty-five men who set sail, only thirty-seven were found. Twenty-three died, and the rest were stuck inside the ship."

"So, what happened to them?"

"Some of the men died before rescuers could cut them out. Others survived but their brains were all gone to mush. Only three or four lived to talk about it."

"What did they say?"

"That the ship had gone into a different place."

"What kind of place?"

"Another world? The electricity and magnetic stuff opened a doorway. The *Eldridge* slipped through the door for thirty seconds, then came back. But something very bad happened in that other place."

"What happened to the men who disappeared?"

Billy opened his eyes. Their convexity reflected the cloudless sky: a glittering, feverish blue. They looked a lot like my uncle's eyes, right then. "The book I read said there were, um, sightings."

"Sightings of what?"

Billy sat up. "Of men who looked just like the ones who had gone missing in that other place, right? Only this was thirty or forty years later. These men—the ones people reported seeing—looked the same as they had on the *Eldridge*. Same age, dressed in old sailor suits. Most times they looked only half there, like ghosts. People saw them around power conductors and dams, places that gave off a lot of electrical or magnetic energy. In dark, lonely places too." Billy swallowed and said, "They were always screaming, or at least their mouths hung open like they were. Except no noise came out."

We sat in silence as wavelets licked the shore.

"I guess your sister doesn't believe in that stuff, huh?"

"Do you like her?"

I had to find somewhere else to look. My cheeks broiled. "No, I just . . ."

"She takes pills."

When I looked back, Billy's mouth was pinched shut. I got the sense he was upset at himself for divulging a family secret.

"I love my sister," Billy said plainly. "But sometimes she—"

Curling his pointer finger around his thumb, Billy popped his thumb up to mimic flicking a switch.

"On, off. Off, on. She can't control it. The pills make her . . . not happy, but not sad either. They make her *less*, yeah? Less Dove." Billy shrugged. "My mom says Dove lives like a sun does. In this never-ending state of heat and light that would burn the rest of us up."

Clouds worked across the sky. Ragged white, they were carried over the water, over Goat Island near the southern shore, giving us fleeting pockets of shade. Billy would find new friends once the summer ended. I understood that. I could even accept it. He was athletic and handsome and broody.

The tremor of the falls carried up the table legs and down my spine. The heartbeat of my city. I hoped Billy could feel it.

When I got home, Mom was smoking a cigarette on the porch. She butted it out when she saw me rounding the corner, waving her hands as if to shoo a fly.

"I'm quitting," she said as I walked my bike up the driveway. "Got to wean myself."

We sat on the steps. She ran her fingers through my hair, brushing my bangs out of my eyes.

"You should wear it to the side, in a part. See more of your face."

I brushed my hair back the way it was and parried her hands away when she tried to finger-comb it again.

"Switching subjects," she said, giving up. "I talked to your uncle today. He said you've made some new friends. A girl, even."

"Mom . . ."

"Only reporting what I've heard."

"She chews tobacco."

"Is that so."

"It smells like cherries."

"Not exactly ladylike."

I thought about Billy asking if I liked Dove. How could I, a mere mortal, *like* Dove Yellowbird? Did mortal men *like* the goddess who lurked in the caldera of their island volcanoes? No, they worshipped those goddesses. If they dared to even think about touching, or kissing, or gazing directly upon the goddess, that goddess would incinerate them like flies in a bug zapper. And those fools would deserve no less.

iv.

I arrived for the first meeting of the Saturday Night Ghost Club at seven o'clock the following evening. Uncle C and Lex Galbraith were waiting inside the Occultorium.

"What did you tell your folks?" my uncle asked.

"I'm spending the night at your house. Watching movies."

"Your father trusts my movie choices again?" he said hopefully.

Jake and Uncle C's Monthly Movie Night had been a regular thing for years, until Uncle C made the mistake of screening *The Mummy*, an old Hammer Horror film. Any other kid would have howled at the cheesy effects and grinding organ soundtrack, but I was traumatized. Thus, Monthly Movie Night had met its abrupt cancellation. Recently my father had grudgingly allowed it to start again, so long as he chose the film.

I unzipped my backpack and showed Uncle C my copy of *The Apple Dumpling Gang*.

"Ugh, VHS." Lex said "VHS" the way other people say *necrotic tissue* or *earwig*. "Inferior in every way. Why make a sandwich with Spam when you could have truffled salami? Why listen to the radio through a pair of tin cans when you could listen through Blaupunkt speakers?"

Billy arrived in pants and a long-sleeved shirt. Uncle C had told us hiking would be involved, and protective clothing was best. I'd only been able to find a turtleneck in my drawers, but Lex, at least, approved of my choice.

"Ah, the noble turtleneck. Classic cool, Jake, old bean. Never goes out of style."

Uncle C slung a backpack over his shoulders. "Let's boogie."

"I'll meet you there," Lex said. "I'm driving, like a civilized human being."

Uncle C, Billy and I popped our kickstands and rode down Portage Road. We charted a course through sleepy suburbs, past packs of boys and girls playing road hockey. Street lights flickered to life as we guided our bikes west down the Haulage Road Trail, past Solar Park where the beer league softball games were going on. Men in bright orange baseball uniforms were clustered around a big cooler in the parking lot, passing the church key, snapping the tops of stubby brown bottles of Labatt's 50.

Haulage Road intersected with Mountain Road. We pedalled along the breakdown lane. Gravel popped under my tires as we followed a razor-wire-topped fence hemming the town's landfill. The greasy stink of trash clung to the air. Crickets leapt from the long grass, kamikaze-style, hitting the spinning spokes on my bike and pelting back into the scrub. The heat died out of the day and my lungs filled with the glorious, crisp, cool evening air.

Then came the pealing *crack!* of a rifle shot. The three of us skidded to a stop.

"I got the bugger!" someone hollered.

A shape crested one of the landfill's toppling slag heaps to stand silhouetted against the sky. A man. Short and barrel-shaped, the dying light reflecting off his teeth. He crouched and picked something up by its tail. A rat as big as a dachshund, or so it seemed to me. The Great White Hunter—otherwise known as one of the dump's guards—swung the dead rat by its tail and hurled it into the fuming waste. He slotted another bullet into his rifle, waved cheerily at us and crow-hopped down the heap out of sight. I figured he'd run out of bullets before killing one-tenth of the rats in the dump. The thought of being surrounded by piles of stinking trash, out of ammo, in a darkness teeming with thousands of pissed-off rats wasn't one I wanted to contemplate.

We swung right on Concession Road 6, skirting the dump. As the street lights became further apart and petered out, we were left to navigate by the glow of the moon. My calves were burning by the time Uncle C eased on his brakes and said, "We'll stash our bikes and walk from here."

We pushed the bikes down to a sheltering glen. My uncle looped a chain between the frames and around a tree, locking them with a padlock. We set off through the brush. Wind hummed around the bark of the maple trees. I became aware of my raspy breath, filling and emptying my lungs. To the west I spotted a house sitting all by itself at the top of a hill.

Billy, walking in front of me, moved with fluid grace. When we came to a tree that had blown over in a storm, he hurdled it effortlessly. I crawled underneath and came up with cockle-burrs stuck to my shirt, which Billy picked off. Funny how meaningful those small tender gestures can be: a friend picking burrs off your shirt, the ones you can't get because they're stuck in that unreachable spot on your back.

The palm-shaped fronds of a walnut tree brushed my face. The hot hum of crickets in my ears. Soon I lost sight of Billy and my uncle, who were moving east while I continued west. Then even the sound of them was gone. Alone in the woods—what could be worse? I imagined owls peering down at me from the crotches of trees . . . would they mistake my sweaty hair, now gummed into gingery ropes, for luscious worms? Would they take flight from their shadowy perches, flap down in a dusty rustling of wings to peck at me, their beaks punching through my skull to get at the wrinkly pink meat of my brain . . . ?

"Jake," Billy called, "over here."

"Coming!"

I rejoined them, and soon the bushes thinned as we came upon some train tracks. The steel was pitted with rust and nettles grew between the ties.

"An old trunk line," my uncle said.

The elongated moon lay trapped within the steel, which bore its light to a vanishing point far west—the rails looked like two infinitely long, wickedly sharp razor blades. The wind gusted down the tracks, making a lonely sound like the howl of a trapped animal.

On the other side of the tracks, a hillside cut down to a path. We followed it to a clearing where Lex waited. He dragged on his cigarette—the ember flared stoplight-red in the dusk—and said, "Booga booga."

"Quit it," my uncle chastised him. "You'll spoil the mood."

We walked to a grove of willows and pushed through their whip-like branches—it was like moving through beaded curtains—until the final leafy drapery parted.

"Welcome to the Screaming Tunnel, boys."

We were standing before Cataract City's most famous haunted spot. My folks had forbidden me from going there—a common decree of all the adults in my town. *Why scare the daylights out of yourself?* went the conventional adult thinking. But my uncle Cal wasn't like most adults.

We faced a tunnel twice as tall as my uncle. With its charred brickwork, its mouth looked like a church's sweeping front door—a church that had nearly burnt to the ground, in this case.

A black church. The church of the Devil.

The tunnel cut through a flat-topped hillside. Metal strips skirted the hilltop—I realized these were the same train tracks we'd crossed earlier. They must bend through the woods to run over the tunnel.

"Let's get a fire going," my uncle said. "And I'll tell you a story."

Wood was plentiful and before long we had a fire. We sat cross-legged, watching each other over the flames.

"There used to be a house over there." My uncle pointed a few degrees north of the tunnel. "A wood-frame jobbie with a croft for two beds. Three people lived in it: a mother, a father, a little girl. The girl was the same age as you boys. The man was a fireman for CP Rail—a *bakehead*, they called those guys. Every week another fireman would show up on a pump trolley on that railroad track up there and take the father to the rail yard off River Road. He'd be gone for days, fighting boxcar fires. I'm told that he . . ."

Uncle C trailed off. After looking at Billy and me in turn, he said, "Guys, this story doesn't have a happy ending. You sure you want to hear it?"

It was just like my uncle to lead you halfway down a lonely road, stop, and ask if you wanted to be there at all. By then you had no choice, did you? He'd brought you there, and he was the only one who knew the way back.

"I'm told he had a temper," my uncle said, picking up his story when he met no objection. "More likely a serious mental disorder, which tended to go undiagnosed in those days. His wife rarely left the home. Their girl was deaf, so the mother home-schooled her. I've heard this story a lot of times from a lot of different people, but I've never heard any names mentioned, just the Man, the Woman and their daughter, the Girl. Every so often they came to town for groceries but otherwise they were not heard from. Until that night, when they became legends."

My uncle paused here to sigh, as if he'd just revealed the saddest fact of all. He hunted a flashlight out of his backpack.

"Let's go take a look, shall we?"

"I'm staying right here," Lex said, staring at Uncle C for a long moment.

It was cool under the trees, and darker with the moon and stars blotted out. A leathery rustle touched my ears . . . suspended from a low branch, hanging like a quivering black nut, was a bat. It spread its wings—I could see moon-glow through their veiny sheerness—and took flight, zizzing past my head, lifting my bangs as it winged past.

We came to a clearing. The mortared outline of an old foundation shone pale blue under the flashlight. Uncle C walked along it, arms out like a performer on a balance beam.

"This is where it happened," he said. A shiver rippled through him.

"A goose must've walked over my grave," he said, but he wasn't smiling. "It happened on a night that was probably not much different than tonight. The man came home after a week of battling blazes on the rails, stinking of smoke and sweat, stepping up the front steps. In that silence, seeping through the door, was a sound rarely heard in the house. I guess you could call it . . . *canoodling*. Breathless little whimpers, giggles, the odd moan."

Uncle C cocked one eyebrow, as perhaps the husband had done himself all those years ago: a viperish and calculating expression.

"The man stood on the porch, listening long enough to confirm his suspicions. All the while, crazed anger boiled within him. He crept to the window. His feet mustn't have made a sound. He peeked through a crack in the curtains. Whatever he saw . . . it was all the push he needed."

Uncle C trained his flashlight thirty yards past the

house. "There used to be a toolshed over there. The man grabbed a can of kerosene and some wedges of scrap lumber. Quickly and quietly, he jammed the wedges under the doors, front and back. He splashed kerosene all about, avoiding the windows—by the time his wife and her lover discovered the house was burning, it'd be too late. When he lit the oil, a ring of flame leapt up. The man stood back, watching it turn to ash: his house, his wife and whoever she was with."

"He burnt them?" Billy's eyes were fixed on my uncle with a metallic sheen. "His own family?"

"The fire rose up, up, up," my uncle said. "The night was alive with it. The poor people inside pounded at the door. The man may've had a weapon, maybe a pitchfork from the shed. When his wife and her lover tried to escape through the shattered windows he could have been outside waiting to stick them with the tines."

I could picture it, though it made me sick—an insane man in greasy overalls hovering outside a busted window, jabbing a pitchfork at the hands of his own wife as she scrabbled frantically to survive.

"The house burnt, yes," my uncle went on. "They were so far out of town that nobody would've seen. At the height of the blaze the front door flew open and the girl stepped out. Her nightgown was ablaze, her body lit like a paper lantern. She was screaming . . .

sometimes people wonder whether a deaf person's screams are the same as someone who can hear, I suppose on account of deaf people not sounding quite the same when they talk. But there's no difference. A scream is a primal sound, and all human screams sound the same. The girl ran down the porch cloaked in fire. She dashed through the swale over there, boys, on into the tunnel. In the centre of the tunnel she let out a final piercing scream."

"She died?" said Billy.

"I'm afraid so."

For all I knew, Uncle C was bullshitting us—no, not bullshitting, because *he* believed this story. But I struggled to remind myself it was just that: a story. Even back then, I was certain that if I were to go to the Niagara Falls library and scan through foot after foot of microfiche of old town records and newspapers, I wouldn't find a shred of evidence to prove this terrible crime had happened. But in that moment, the story *felt* true: the mossy mortared foundation shone phantom blue under my uncle's flashlight, illuminating the undeniable fact that a home had once stood right there. Closing my eyes, I could hear the delirium-filled breaths as the man observed his wife and her lover through the parted curtains—I could *hear* his voice, gravelly with rage and holding a tinselly note of madness, right next to my ear.

"The man was arrested," my uncle went on. "Sent off to prison, maybe the funny farm. The wife and her lover, the girl . . . all of them died. And that tunnel," Uncle C said, "became the Screaming Tunnel. Now the legend is, if you go into the tunnel and strike a match on the stroke of midnight, you'll see the girl standing right in front of you, watching you. Then the match will go out, even if there's not a hint of breeze. Then . . . it's just you and her in the dark together."

"Quit it," I said.

Uncle C laughed. "Listen, I'm only telling you the legend."

We walked back to the fire. I cut my eyes at Billy to gauge whether he was as freaked as I was. Now Uncle C was whistling. The sound started low and rose to a high pitch like the scream of a train whistle . . . or of a little girl on fire. I wanted to tell him to stop it, to shut up—*SHUT UP, CALVIN!*—using his first name to shock him.

Back at the fire Lex had whittled sticks. He skewered a marshmallow on each and passed them around. Our marshmallows bobbed above the wagging flames. Mine caught on fire and the gelatin hissed as it incinerated—unsurprisingly, it sounded as if the marshmallow was screaming.

We ate marshmallows and drank the cans of Pepsi that Lex had brought. Lex opened his cigarette pack and produced a funny-looking one. He lit it and inhaled, blowing the smoke away from us. I still caught its scent—the same as the air under the high school football bleachers.

"Oh, for Pete's sake," my uncle said.

Lex's chin jutted. "You drag me out here in the dead of night—can't I have any fun at all?"

"Go into the woods, if you insist."

Lex heaved himself up and slouched off to a stand of elms twenty feet away.

"Go further," Uncle C said.

"Go to hell," Lex said, staying where he was.

While Lex smoked, Uncle C amused Billy and me with an item that had recently come in over the Bat Phone.

"Got word of a fellow down in Rosalita, Texas. A man of a superstitious disposition who drove around with one of those plastic Jesuses stuck to the dashboard of his Chevy Coupe de Ville. Some fellas prefer a hula girl or a bobbly-headed dog, but this guy went with his personal Lord and Saviour. He gets into a head-on collision and wouldn't you know it—that plastic Jesus flies off the dashboard, pierces his chest and kills him dead. And *that* is why you will never find any religious iconography in my proximity."

Lex came back radish-eyed and giggly. He began to eat marshmallows directly from the bag with cheerful determination. The night stilled. The industry of the nocturnal creatures diminished, as if they too were aware of the approaching midnight hour. A freshet of water spewed from the pipe projecting from the bricks near the tunnel, releasing a fungal odour.

Uncle C checked his watch. "Time to see if the legend is true."

He unzipped his backpack and produced a pack of wooden fireplace matches: six inches long with blue phosphorus tips.

Lex said, "Oh, Cal. Really? You'll scare the bloody daylights out of them."

"I want to do it," Billy said.

"What about you, Jake?" Lex said.

When I hesitated, Billy rested his hand on my shoulder.

"It's called the Ghost Club, Jake. Right?"

Billy's eyes shone with excitement. They were the eyes of a boy who'd gleefully stick his head into a tiger's mouth just to breathe in the raw meat on its breath.

My memory of the following few minutes is troubled. Remembering it now is like trying to re-create a dream. I can remember walking towards the tunnel. My uncle was in the lead, then Lex, then Billy, then me. It seemed as if all the elements of night had concentrated into a knot of impenetrable dark at the mouth of the tunnel, even darker than the blackness between the stars.

Lex said, "Give us some damn light, Cal."

The flashlight played over a stream of brackish water trickling down to the tunnel opening . . . but the light failed to penetrate into the tunnel itself, which was hung with vaporous shadows. I glanced back at the fire but it seemed a thousand miles away, nothing but a quivering orange dot, and when I turned back towards the dark it was like one of those cinematic smash-zooms—suddenly I was inside the tunnel. The belly of the beast.

Lex said, "Hello-ello-ello . . . *ello*? Anybody home-ome-ome-ome?"

Our footsteps echoed in the emptiness. My mind circled back to the girl. If she appeared, what would she look like? Young and milky-skinned, or charred like a pot roast left too long in the oven? Maybe just a struggling heap of melted skin and bone? If she still had a face, would she gaze at us forlornly—or smile, grateful for the company? Maybe she'd reach for me, beseeching me to stay with her forever in the dark.

These morbid thoughts filtered down from my skull to pollute the rest of my body. I wanted nothing to do with her eternal misery—it seemed invasive and cruel to even seek sight of her, no different from going to a prison to gawp at a wrongly convicted man.

We reached the middle of the tunnel. Water dripped all around us with the clatter of rain-bleached bones. Uncle C removed the matches from his pocket while I held the flashlight.

"Everyone ready?"

We huddled in a circle. We could have been at the bottom of the sea.

"Turn off the flashlight," my uncle commanded.

Half-heartedly, I did. My heart was pounding so hard that I could hear the blood-beat in my ears. My uncle's hand closed over mine, his fingers knitting up with my own.

"It's okay," he whispered. "She's as scared as we are."

The match flared. The air was bathed in its light. In its flickering radius, the darkness trickled away from something hunched a few feet in front of us— it was as if the darkness itself was fleeing from that billowing form—

A shape came together, or so it seemed to my twelve-year-old eyes. The outline of a body draped all in white, the chalky edge of a nightgown fluttering in an unfelt breeze, or no, it was fire, ghostly white fire, stirring along the ground. My eyes rose against their will as if my eyelids had been pierced with fish-hooks and dragged upwards to behold a face—or so I could've sworn—a deathless young-old face with the remnants of bygone prettiness, staring at me with sad yet ancient eyes as she reached a skeletal hand towards my face. . . .

Mine . . . stay, play . . . all *mine* . . .

A thundering clatter arose from someplace above. The match was snuffed out.

v.

I came to outside the tunnel.

"You fainted," said Billy.

I stared up at a ring of faces. I couldn't remember what . . . some sort of apparition, or was it . . . ? Apparently my eyes had rolled back in my head as my legs went out from under me. My uncle had caught me in the dark. I retained the sense-memory of his arms enfolding me. He must have carried me out, too, like a sack of flour.

As consciousness seeped back in, so too did my shame . . . how could I be such a baby?

"You okay?" Billy asked.

"Yeah, I . . . I just—"

"I saw her, too," Billy said.

In silence, we doused the fire and bundled into Lex's van. Lex stopped a few miles up the road, where Billy and my uncle hopped out to retrieve our bikes, then hopped back in. We drove to town. I had to clench my jaw to avoid bursting into tears—and it was more than the burning shame of fainting dead away. Had we really seen her? Lex claimed he'd witnessed nothing. My uncle copped to glimpsing a pale flicker, nothing definite. The clatter, they said, must have been made by a maintenance train passing over the trestle . . . except we all knew those tracks hadn't been in use for years.

Lex dropped off Billy at his house. Billy gave me a look of cautious concern and said, "Want to hang out tomorrow?"

I shrugged, noncommittal.

Lex dropped me and Uncle C at my uncle's house. I got out of the van, zombie-like. "You okay, Jacob?" Lex asked.

I smiled stiffly. "I'm fine."

"You'll sleep it off," he assured me.

I pushed my bike up the walk while Lex spoke to my uncle. When he drove off, the tires of his van made a scalded-cat screech. Uncle C caught up to me at the door and offered a strained smile. I couldn't tell if he was commiserating with me for what had happened, admitting some guilt on his end, or was ashamed of me for fainting but didn't want me to catch on.

He let us in and switched on the kitchen lights. "Want some warm milk, Jake? Help you sleep."

I shook my head no.

My uncle stared out the window overlooking his backyard. I followed his gaze. The mulberry tree in the centre of the lawn looked like a hooded executioner slouching towards the chopping block.

"I'm sorry if . . . I thought if you and I faced it together . . ."

"It's okay."

"Really?"

"Yeah, really." But I wasn't so sure if that was the truth.

"Go on to bed, Jake. I made up the bed with fresh sheets."

The spare room was cluttered with overstock from the Occultorium: boxes marked SORCERER STUFF and VARIOUS MAJICKS or RUBE JUNK. I crawled under the covers of the bed and stared at the ceiling. Uncle C had drawn designs up there with glow-in-the-dark paint. Symbols my uncle said had protective powers against nightmares and dream-stealing imps.

I awoke at the witching hour. Down the hallway, in some other part of the house, I heard weeping. It was Uncle C. After a while, his thick cries trailed into a guttural sob. I'd never heard anyone make a sound like that. It was a noise more animal than human.

I got out of bed. After spending many nights in my

uncle's house, I knew the boards that creaked and all the dead spots on the floor. I crept silently down the hall to the kitchen, where my uncle sat at the table. Moonlight fell through the window, scalloping his heaving chest. There was a sheaf of paper on the table, and charcoal pencils like the ones I used in art class. He was doing something with his hands, which lay trapped in the moonlight—miming the movement of letting someone's hair fall through his fingers, again and again.

"Where did it go?"

Those words, piercingly clear, were spoken in a voice so unlike my uncle's that I thought someone else must be sitting in that kitchen chair: my uncle's ruined doppelgänger.

"Where did it all go?"

I stood in the hallway, unable to offer my uncle any comfort for his wretched need. I understand now that I was just a kid, at that stage where we're good at forcing others to deal with our own outbursts but less adept when dealing with the painful emotions of others. I had no idea how to help, and . . . and I was so scared.

There it was again, that animal sob. I pictured dozens of tiny mouths over every square inch of my uncle's skin, mouths puckering on his arms and legs and chest, all of them twisted open and wailing.

I snuck back to my bed, where I lay shaking. Eventually I drifted off, but woke again to glimpse my uncle in the darkness of the room. His head floated like a disembodied oracle in the doorway, his eyes unfocused while his jaw worked around words he could not speak. . . . Now, all these years later, I choose to remember that as only another dream.

In the morning, I got dressed and walked past my uncle's bedroom. He was fast asleep. His big pelican-like feet jutted off the bed, his toes furred with baby-ish blond hair.

Sunlight filled the kitchen. The drawings my uncle had done in the dead of night were spread on the table. Knowing it was invasive but unable to help myself, I leafed through them.

First was a woman's face. Her features were indistinct, trapped in shadows created with subtle strokes of charcoal. It was almost as if he'd sketched her from the bottom of a lake, peering up through the water to capture the face as it danced above the surface.

The next drawing was more concrete. The interplay of white and black along the top of the page gave the impression of trees: closely-knit pines arrayed like the teeth on a saw. A box at the bottom right represented a dwelling. The trees were scaled back to an eerie polar whiteness in the centre of the frame. There, a skeletal and famished shape hunched towards the house: some creature breaching the shadowy recesses of the woods to forge boldly into the light. I thought of the thing Billy talked about, the Windiigog. Wendigo. Eater of human flesh.

I flipped the sheaf over to the last sketch. . . .

The leering, hate-filled face of a demon. It filled the page. Its features were rendered in brutal slashes, and its teeth were glints of busted glass crowded into its mouth. Its eyes just black pits—my uncle's frenzied strokes had ripped coin-sized holes where the irises should have been.

This is from the Void, was my thought. *Wherever the USS* Eldridge *had disappeared into.*

The face belonged to a creature that could only exist in a gap between worlds—the same gap as the one the doomed destroyer had slipped inside. It belonged to something that lurked in the green mists, waiting for its prey to stumble along so it could steal their sanity and soul. An even more worrisome thought branched off this one: perhaps it wasn't the face of a demon at all. Maybe I was looking at a man who'd been stuck in that gap for too long. Who had surrendered his elemental humanity, whose mouth hung open in an endless scream.

Fingers shaking, I pulled a clean sheet of paper over that hideous face. Walking to the mud room, I pulled my shoes on and slipped out the door without waking my uncle.

Years later, I can see how things might have ended there, if only I had put one of those drawings in my pocket and showed it to my parents. But at the time, I couldn't allow myself to do that. These drawings were the product of my uncle's secret heart. In my own naïveté, I felt that to take one would have been to snatch part of his soul.

I would think about my uncle's drawings when I saw the paintings of my young patient: Gunther and Camphor, robot and druid, were the fruits of her own secret heart. The girl had found them—two pulsing blips of familiar, loving light—within the dimming corridors of her brain. Found them, or summoned them at the time of greatest need. They stood as proof that her memories were still there, very faint, but persistent.

4.

SUNKEN WRECK

S ilas Gibbons was a louse. He knew it. Everyone who knew him knew it.

Games of chance were his poison. Cards, dice, the ponies. Gambling alters the brain's chemistry: there is a massive dopamine output when the dealer goes bust in Blackjack or the filly you're betting on wins by a nose. This is offset by the crash when it is you who goes bust—but the brains of hardened addicts are conditioned to push past such minor setbacks.

Silas's gambling encouraged the usual related issues. He lived alone and had the eating habits of a college student. He dated fellow card sharps who operated on similar skeleton-shift hours: the casino was open all night and Silas could be found there at the witching hour, slinging cards with the other railbirds. He was in debt to everyone in his family and several ex-friends. If he felt guilt or shame over this, it wasn't enough to compel him to quit.

But in his mid-thirties, Silas changed, for no reason that anyone could see. He hadn't hit rock bottom. Bookies would still take his markers. Even Silas couldn't account for the change. He simply didn't want to live that way anymore.

"It was like eating too much cotton candy," he told me during our initial consultation. "I just . . . I got sick of it."

Silas took a regular job. He joined a gym and acquainted himself with the produce section at the supermarket. He made amends with those he'd cheated during his "bad years." He met someone he wanted to marry. A year after the wedding, his wife gave birth to a girl.

Six weeks after his daughter's birth, Silas began to experience crippling migraines. Three weeks later, he was on my table.

The tumour was an adenoma on his pituitary gland, lodged in the folds of the corpus callosum. It was the largest such tumour I'd seen, but benign.

The operation was routine. The tumour came out in one solid mass. Two days later, Silas was on his feet again.

The next week, after his daughter was asleep in her crib, Silas told his wife he was heading to the gym. Instead, he went to the casino.

He kept his lapses discreet for the next month. A few hours, a few hundred dollars won or lost, then back home with his wife none the wiser. Why would she look for signs? The old Silas, the bad one, was only a rumour to her. Steadily, his habit worsened. He began to disappear all night. His wife was outraged. She wouldn't stand for it, shouldn't have to. Silas showed up for work with bloodshot eyes, wearing his rumpled card-playing clothes. He lost his job, but being fired didn't perturb him. Shortly after that, his wife moved out and took their daughter.

Silas Gibbons was a full-on louse again. The transformation had taken less than three months.

I had no contact with Silas during this time: the operation had been open-and-shut, no follow-up required. But five years later, he walked back into my office and told me his story.

He looked healthy. He said he'd recently joined the gym and was eating well. His wife had divorced him—"She had every right to"—but he declared he was newly dedicated to winning her back. So far, this plan wasn't working, though she had thawed. She was letting him see his daughter for a few hours every second weekend.

"But the headaches," he said. "They're killing me."

An MRI disclosed the obvious. The tumour had come back. Benign tumours often regrow in the same spot, like a fruiting potato.

"It's easy enough to get rid of it again," I told him. "This time I can clean it up, dig out all the clinging threads and—"

Silas set his palms on my desk. "No."

"No?"

"I need it."

"That's interesting, Silas. Why do you think that?"

"I think . . . I think I'm a better person with it in my brain."

I considered his theory. The tumour's placement indicated that it did indeed press against a primary impulse centre. And Silas's personality adjustment had occurred over several years that coincided with the growth of the tumour in his brain. Was it possible that the tumour was the equivalent of the little Dutch boy's finger in the dike, blocking addictions that governed Silas's life? When I'd excised it years ago, had the absence caused those compulsions to come back? Clearly Silas thought so. He also believed his problems would return if I removed this new growth.

The tumour wasn't getting any bigger. I gave Silas a choice. "We can leave it in, but I'll have to monitor it. The migraines will continue."

"Anything. Just leave it be."

I prescribed medication. If he felt a migraine coming on, he popped a pill. If he got ahead of it, he was often fine. If not, he crawled into bed and turned off the lights and suffered. If this was his penance, Silas was willing to serve it.

In time, his wife took him back. By now, their daughter would be nine. And that tumour remains in Silas's brain.

i.

I spent the days following the Screaming Tunnel episode moping around the house. I watched so much TV in the sun-heated family room that my body welded to the leather couch, and I had to peel myself off like a giant Band-Aid. My folks didn't ask me about that night at Uncle C's. So far as they knew, I'd spent it watching an old Bill Bixby flick. And my uncle didn't reach out to offer an apology beyond the one he'd given. Why should he? It had been my choice to go along with the club.

About a week later, I was sitting on the porch reading a *G.I. Joe* comic when Dove Yellowbird rode up.

"Howdy, stranger."

"Hey. How . . . ?"

"Do I know where you live? I have eyes all over, grasshopper. Not *actually*, you understand—eyes all over my body would be incredibly gross. It's just a turn of phrase."

She popped a wheelie over the curb and sent her bike ghost-riding towards the elm in our front yard, into which it crashed. Dove wore cut-off shorts, a ball cap and a plain white T. "Haven't seen you around lately."

I offered what I hoped was a carefree shrug. "Just doing stuff around home."

"Uh-huh. That's about the size of it, I'm sure. Go for a ride?"

Her request went through my body like music, a chord struck just for me. I got my bike out of the garage. We rode down to Menzie Street, which emptied onto Stanley. The Fairview Cemetery spread out to our right, its hillsides lined with tombstones and Great War cenotaphs. Dove rode no-hands, her hair fanning out in the wind like the tail feathers of some wonderful bird.

"I hear you went to some tunnels? Billy told me he was scared silly." She spat a stream of tobacco juice in a graceful arc. "I mean, some creepy old tunnel in the dead of night. Who wouldn't be terrified?"

We rode through the intersection at Roberts Avenue into the tourist zone. Billy was waiting for us on the corner of Lewis Avenue. He and I nodded at each other, then together the three of us rode to the Occultorium. It felt like a natural destination, although I still wasn't sure I was ready to face my uncle.

Thankfully, the shop was closed. So Beta! was open, though not a single customer populated its aisles. Lex lounged out front smoking a cigarette.

"Want to rent something? On the house."

"We have a VHS player," Dove told him.

Lex's face crumpled like a paper bag.

"Looking for your uncle?" he asked me. "Been a while since I've seen him."

That wasn't unusual. My uncle often got wound up by something he'd heard over the Bat Phone and was liable to shut down the shop for a few days.

"Hey, Ghostbusters," Lex said to us. "Looking for another case?"

"Not me," said Dove. "Places to go, people to see."

At that, Dove popped her front tire up and cat-walked down the sidewalk, wending between the sloth-like tourists. The trailing fringe of her hair whisked around the street corner, leaving only the smell of cherries in the air.

Following Dove's departure, Lex said, "Well, what about you two goons? I want you to recover something of mine. From a witch."

"Get out of town," I said.

Lex's tongue prodded at his canine tooth. "Okay, she's my ex-girlfriend. But witches come in all shapes and sizes."

Billy said, "What did she do to you?"

"You mean besides rip my heart out and stomp on it? She kept my cat."

He went in and came back with a photo. It showed a man, a woman and a cat. The woman was young and smiling. The man was also smiling. It took me a moment to register that the man was Lex, whom I'd always known to be basset-faced and dour. Maybe his ex *was* a witch. She appeared to have laid a curse on him, turning him from the man in the photo into . . . *Lex*.

"That's her." Lex pointed at the cat. "Becca. Best cat in the world. The breakup was a disaster. She booted me out in the dead of night and I came back next morning to find my stuff strewn across the lawn. All my worldly possessions, except Becca."

"Why not just ask for her back?" said Billy.

"You think I haven't tried?" Lex said. "My ex is an unreasonable entity."

I said, "You sound like you really don't like her."

Lex set his jaw, then let it relax. "Ah, we both made mistakes. Water under the bridge, che serà, serà. But she won't give me back my cat—and that is witchy, don't you think?"

Billy said, "How much is the cat worth to you?"

"Shrewd, my young sir. *Shrewd*."

Lex offered a ten-dollar retrieval fee, plus an additional dollar for incidentals.

Billy agreed to the terms, gave me my half and tucked the remainder into his pocket.

Then he said, "You still got Becca's cat-carrier, Mr. Galbraith?"

ii.

We arrived at the witch's house with the cat-carrier bouncing off Billy's handlebars. Along the way, we had stopped at the pet store for a bag of catnip, burning through half of our incidentals.

The house didn't look like it belonged to a witch. It was painted a cheery shade of robin's-egg blue, with white shutters. The lawn did not appear to have a patch of eye-of-newt or wolfsbane. I did, however, notice a hearse parked down the road, which I was fairly certain belonged to the undertaker Stanley Rowe.

We stashed our bikes behind the hedge and walked up the drive. Billy unlatched the gate. We crept into the backyard, where a window looked in on the kitchen.

"I'm pretty good at trapping," Billy whispered. "Marten, porcupine. My uncles taught me."

"We won't hurt her, right?"

"No, no."

A square was set into the bottom of the back door, draped by a rubber flap. A cat door. Billy lifted it and made a whispering noise—*wsswsswsswss.* . . .

He set the flap back softly. "Her head's poking around the corner of the kitchen. But we can't throw the catnip in. She'll just play with it and not come out."

"What about our shoelaces?"

"Perfect."

We stripped the laces from our sneakers, and I knotted them together into a long string. Billy tied the catnip Baggie to one end.

"Lift the flap, Jake," he told me.

Billy swung the string like a lasso and tossed the Baggie through the flap.

"She's interested," he reported, jigging the string the way a fisherman works his line to coax a fish to bite. "She's taking a sniff. Come on . . . a little closer . . ."

"Oh God, *yeeeeesss!*"

The euphoric cry came from the upper floor of

the house. This was followed by a full-throated rumble like a grizzly bear awakening from hibernation—except there was *joy* in that sound, a tidal wave of pleasure so all-consuming, so gratified, that it was scary.

Billy and I exchanged an anxious glance. Next, we heard footsteps.

"Oh dang," Billy hissed as he reeled in the string.

No sooner had the cat door settled in place than a man padded into the kitchen. I recognized Stanley Rowe, in nothing but boxer shorts and tube socks. I was shocked at how extraordinarily hairy he was, and he was smiling, an expression I'd never known to grace the undertaker's face. Yes, Stanley Rowe was grinning like a schoolboy, one sock yanked up to his knee and the other wadded around his ankle like a half-shed snakeskin. I recall thinking how beautiful he looked. Not physically—Stan Rowe didn't have that in him, not with his keratin-deprived skin and galumphing body—but his happiness made him beautiful in that moment.

Billy and I crouched on the other side of the door with our eyes just above the windowsill while Mr. Rowe opened the fridge and slugged down orange juice straight from the jug.

"You want anything, Janet?" he called.

"Just you back in my sweet lovin' arms!"

Billy and I exchanged glances. The woman's voice must belong to Lex's ex. The witch.

Mr. Rowe chuckled. "You're a lucky man, Stan." He shut the fridge and loafed back upstairs. "Lucky, lucky man."

Once he was gone, we dissolved into a fit of giggles. The sight of Stanley Rowe in his underwear was insanely funny. My chest felt like it was going to splinter, I was struggling so hard to keep my laughter in.

"See how hairy he was?" Billy whispered.

"Like a bear," I said. "Or a sweater he can't take off."

We gulped huge whoofs of air to tamp down our mirth and went back to work. I lifted the cat-door flap so Billy could sling the bag in. Working cautiously, he lured the cat outside. Becca was a slender calico, pie-eyed and drooling from the 'nip. When I picked her up she purred, kneading my shirt with her paws.

We slipped through the gate to our bikes, the tongues of our lace-less Converses whapping our ankles. Becca went into the carrier without a fuss. We rode away like bandits.

Back at So Beta!, Lex melted at the sight of his long-lost cat.

"You little twerps actually pulled it off." There was rare delight in Lex's voice as he cooed, "My Becca, my little Becca the boo."

The cat seemed happy enough to see him. My impression of cats was that you could be the Malibu Strangler and so long as you fed and fussed over them, most would tolerate your company. I felt bad for Janet, who would soon find Becca missing. But according to Lex, it had been his cat all along, so all we'd done was enforce his right of ownership.

We were re-stringing our shoes when Uncle C stepped into So Beta! He checked up, not expecting to find us there, but his face broke into an easy grin.

"How are you, my dear boys?"

After an awkward silence, Lex said, "They got Becca back for me."

"How did you manage it?" When neither Billy nor I piped up, Uncle C offered a wry wink. "Ah. I see. Trade secrets."

With that wink, the chill between us melted away so quickly that I could hardly remember having felt it in the first place.

"Now, boys," Uncle C said, "I've been thinking about the next meeting of our little club—"

Lex said, "Is that still going on?"

"Why ever not, Lex?"

"Oh, I don't know, Cal. Maybe because . . ." Lex trailed off, thinking better of whatever reservation he had been set to lodge. Uncle C faced Billy and me, focusing his full attention on us. It was unnerving, those twin balls of light blazing in his eye sockets.

"I propose a daytime excursion to a sunken wreck. A car abandoned in a shallow oxbow lake off the Niagara River."

If I'd been watching Lex right then, I'd no doubt have seen the blood drain out of his face. But my attention was on Uncle C.

"A car?" said Lex. "Where did you say it was?"

"West of town. I know the place."

"Do you? . . . Cal, what happened there?"

"An accident," Uncle C said. "A car ran off a bridge. Someone drowned."

Lex let his head drop. "This town's full of sorrows, isn't it?"

"I suppose so," said Uncle C, as if he'd never thought about it until then.

"You really think we ought to go, Cal? Considering how it all went at the tunnel?"

"Lex, you've got goosebumps." My uncle gave his old friend a thunderous clap on the back. "You're just not built for this paranormal stuff, are you?"

"Is the sunken car haunted?" I asked.

"That is for us to investigate. But we'll do it in daylight. Take a break from the moonlit ghost hunts. Who's in?"

"Me," Billy said immediately. After a pause, I nodded.

"And you, Lexington?"

"I'll think about it."

Uncle C gave him a smile as big as all outdoors. "The opportunity awaits."

iii.

The following Saturday, the morning air held a hazy effervescence. I'd already shoved my snorkel and mask in my backpack and was in the kitchen making a PB&J sandwich when Dad came downstairs.

"Where are you off to this fine day?"

"Out with Uncle C and Billy."

Dad thumbed a shard of sleep-crust from the corner of his eye. "Be safe. A lot of Bigfoot sightings hereabouts. The Loch Ness Monster's cousin is lurking in the Niagara River, too."

"*Dad.*"

"Only reporting what I've heard."

The neighbourhood was waking up as I pedalled down the street. Sunshine hung in lambent curtains over the lawns. I imagined the heat circling like a restless buzzard: present, waiting, but not yet touching down.

Uncle C waited in front of the Occultorium. Lex

wasn't with him. Shouldering a huge backpack, he said, "Let us venture boldly forth."

We rode down Clifton Hill. My uncle slalomed between the parking meters—the one time Uncle C looked graceful was when he was straddling a bike, where his limbs took on a heron-like elegance. We continued to the Niagara Parkway edging the river. The water shone through stands of poplar; the river was wide and sleek, mirror-calm on its surface while below, I knew, it rushed with furious menace.

The sun was starting to throw corridors of heat down the streets. Strips of hot-patch softened into gummy ribbons that sucked at my bike tires. We pedalled to the bend at Burning Spring Hill to reach Dufferin Island. The slack water ringing the island flowed into a series of oxbows, or small lakes created by water spilling over the riverbanks. They were shallow, warm, and we local kids got territorial over them. Certain clubs or groups of kids were known to colonize a given oxbow, turning it into a private fiefdom. It could get so that trying to swim in a "marked" oxbow was to invite a fist fight.

The oxbow we stopped at was the largest of the chain, too big for anybody to claim feudal rights. A bridge had once spanned it. Rusted jags of rebar snaked from crumbling concrete on the opposing shores.

The lake was quiet when we showed up, but as the day wore on the oxbow's banks would collect families and young lovers and anglers with a taste for catfish. My uncle and I had staked out a spot on the shore when Billy showed up with Dove. My uncle unzipped his massive backpack and hauled out a dinghy. The black plastic was festooned with PVC patches, their edges bubbled with contact cement.

"She's seaworthy, I promise," my uncle said, inflating it with a foot-bellows.

It wouldn't be a disaster if the dinghy sank. Oxbows rarely rose above neck-deep, except in their middle where they might dip to ten. Dove kicked off her shoes and dug her toes into the lake bank. The alluvial soil had a claylike feel under your toes.

Dove yanked a foot back. "*Sheeeeeee—*it."

Her toe had been cut on a shard of glass from a shattered, buried Coke bottle. It was a grazing incision that could have been made by a surgeon's scalpel. A line of blood leaked from it, the red stark against her skin. We sat there, everyone looking at the cut, just watching Dove bleed for a moment.

Then my uncle said, "Heeeeeead 'em up, mooooove 'em out!"

We dragged the dinghy down to the shore and tossed in our gear. The three of us kids straddled the gunwale as Uncle C waded out until the dinghy floated free, then we all hopped aboard. We sat with our backs against the rubber, inhaling the summery wet-inner-tube smell. Beads of water clung to Dove's leg just above her kneecap. Each bead was swollen, almost too big, seven or eight beads spaced like an undiscovered constellation on Dove's thigh, the sun's light bending through each one to create a trembling rainbow. . . . I realized that I'd been staring, transfixed, and when I glanced up Dove was scrutinizing me with her head tilted to the side, her face set in an expression somewhere between curiosity and mirth.

"There's a car out here." My uncle pointed to the vague middle of the oxbow. "What happened was . . . first, let me set the scene. It was night, they say."

"They who?" Dove asked.

"They who first told the story, those whose names are lost to the mists of time." My uncle grinned. "Good enough?"

"If they say so, Calvin."

"Oh, they do," my uncle said. "The car spun out on black ice, crashed through the guardrail, went off the bridge that once spanned this lake. It crashed through the ice and sunk. The two passengers died. A father and his daughter. They tried to unroll the windows but the electrical system had shorted out. They both drowned."

This was hard to imagine on a bright summer day, but a scenario gradually formed in my mind: A winter night, the air flurrying with snow. A father and his daughter in their car, poking down the road. Maybe they'd been coming home from someplace ... the Christmas tree farm over in Douglastown? Returning now in a warm car, sipping the spiced cider they'd bought from the little stand at the farmhouse. Then the tires lose traction, the car fishtails, slews, smashes through the rail, and for a moment there's that sick weightless feeling you get on an amusement park ride—*flutter-guts*, my mother called it. Next, they're crashing through the ice, which splinters with a squeaky-grindy sound, an ozonated taste hitting the back of their throats as the electrical system is fried by the inrushing water. And they sink, settling down to the bottom of the oxbow, the darkness of the water deeper than night. Maybe fish had darted past the windows in sleek quicksilver flashes. Maybe they had clawed at the windows, tearing their fingernails out, perhaps the father tried to smash the glass and push his daughter towards the surface but the water would've been awfully cold, and anyway, the car could have sunk on an angle—the girl could have kicked straight up only to hit a plate of ice.

Dove said, "Their bodies aren't still inside, are they?"

"I don't know what happened to them . . ." Uncle C trailed off, his eyes stuck somewhere above the tree-tops. "Stanley Rowe took them, I'm sure. Stan takes everyone who passes on around here, doesn't he?"

I said, "Why hasn't anyone pulled the car out of the lake?"

My uncle said, "Good question. But you've lived here your whole life, Jake."

I understood what he meant. Like the derelict buildings that were never torn down, the abandoned shopping carts that rusted away to atoms, and all the other monuments to the city's general apathy, the car in the oxbow had become an accepted part of the scenery.

"The legend is that, some days, you can see the girl floating above the water. It happens when day's shading into evening—in that ashy light. Suspended there, mist in the form of a girl hanging a foot or so above the water."

"How does she look?"

"How do you mean, Jake?"

"He means," Dove said to Uncle C, "does she look like she did before the accident, or how she looked after?"

She was right. I didn't want to see a poor creature like the girl in the Screaming Tunnel—in this case, a girl with saggy waterlogged skin and crayfish jostling inside her mouth.

"I don't know how she'd look." My uncle lowered his eyes, tracking the water lapping against the dinghy. "I don't know if there's even any truth to the story."

Billy asked, "Is she a ghost?"

"If she exists at all," my uncle said, "she may be a preta. What are known as hungry ghosts. I've heard them described as humanoid, but with shrivelled, mummified skin, spindly limbs, long thin necks— almost giraffe-like. Giant bellies and small, sucked-in mouths. Hungry ghosts are born when a person dies wanting something, be it love or hope or sanity. That's why they have slender necks and gigantic bellies. Pretas have enormous appetites but lack the ability to satisfy them."

"What could the girl have died in want of?" Dove said.

"It could be something physical. She must've died in want of air. That seems the most likely, doesn't it?"

Hungry ghost. I was one hundred percent convinced I didn't want to see one of those.

"Pretas exist in torment, but it's a gentle torment," Uncle C went on. "They're ghosts, after all. They don't feel the same things we do—not with the same intensity as when they were alive. Their bodies are insubstantial and their emotions are, too . . . wait a sec . . . look, *there*, I see it."

Sunlight petalled through the water, creating lit shelves where it reflected off the silt, the light daggering down to flash off the sunken car. The metal seemed too close to the surface, somehow, hovering a mere foot below the water. Billy must've had this same sense. He dipped his fingers into the lake hesitantly, figuring he'd touch whatever was there, but his hand went in to the wrist and then the elbow before he pulled it out.

"You'll have to dive down to it," my uncle said.

Dove peeled her T-shirt over her head in one smooth motion. Her violet one-piece bathing suit glittered like fish scales and I could see the supple workings of her tendons through the fabric. The way she did this everyday action—so casually, as though she was undressing alone in her bedroom—was breathtaking in a way my twelve-year-old mind couldn't fully comprehend.

I wriggled out of my shorts down to my swim trunks. My thighs squeaked on the rubber bottom of the dinghy. I didn't want Dove to see my pasty rotundness, the belly overhanging my trunks. By the time I'd struggled out of my shirt Billy and Dove were in the water, where they swam with easy grace. Billy generated fantastic momentum with the slightest scissoring of his legs. Dove lazed on her back, arms outspread, luxuriating in the sun.

I pulled on my dive mask and adjusted my snorkel. The mask pinched my vision inwards—so much that I overbalanced and pitched forward with my arms oaring wildly, caught my foot on the rigging rope and fell face-first into the water. Water rocketed up my nose.

"You are a great many things, nephew of mine," my uncle said once I'd surfaced, "but light on your feet isn't one of them."

We gathered in a rough ring, treading water above the car. Dove exhaled and let herself sink. Her chin dipped beneath the surface as her mouth filled with water. She spat it out in a stream and said, "I'm touching it. The roof, with my big toe."

Knowing that the car was so close only amplified the tragedy. The length of Dove Yellowbird's stretched-out body: that was the distance that had separated those two souls from their needless deaths. I cast an anxious glance at Uncle C, but his eyes were riveted to the sky. His chest moved visibly in and out, as if he was struggling to breathe.

"Uncle C?"

"Go," he said, eyes still looking skyward while his fingers clutched the rigging lines of the dinghy. "Go on down and take a look. But *carefully*."

The three of us submerged. The water was clear, the view through my goggles glasslike. The car was sunk to its wheel wells in the bottom of the oxbow. Its paint job was perfectly preserved; it could have recently rolled off the factory floor. Air bubbles jetted from Dove's nostrils and corkscrewed to the surface. My ears popped—the sound a *crunch* inside my skull.

Billy gripped the window frame and levered his head through the passenger side. Dove crossed her legs and let her body drop until she settled near the lake bottom. The Yellowbirds' eyes ticked here and there, taking everything in. When I saw no fear in their gazes, I kicked down to join them. My hands settled around the window frame. I flexed my arms, trying to pull myself down—Billy gripped my legs and pulled until I was next to him.

The car was eerily intact. The seats were un-ripped, the dashboard in showroom condition. It reminded me of the ant frozen in amber that my mom sometimes wore around her neck: an ant that had died a million years ago. If I were to turn the keys in the ignition—and they were still there, attached by a foam boat key chain, which struck me as a horrible irony—it seemed conceivable the car would start, its headlights burning holes through the water.

Even now, I can remember the small details. How the wipers had stopped halfway up the windshield, mid-wipe, the rubber chewed away by sunfish. Crayfish daisy-chaining from the open glovebox, linked pincer to pincer. The scene looked peaceful. There was nothing bloody inside that vehicle. It was like touring an old battlefield. The water and Father Time had cleansed the car of its horrors. But somewhere, nibbling at a recessed part of my brain, sat the knowledge that people had died here. The car was sanitized now, no different from a crime scene once the photos have been snapped and the chalk outlines washed away—but the psychic resonance persisted.

My lungs throbbed for air. I pushed off the bottom and kicked. Dove and Billy did the same. Our bodies speared the water's surface. I floated, breathing raggedly, shards of prismatic light in my eyes.

"Well?" my uncle said.

My eyes met Dove's, synced, and we came to an immediate understanding.

"It's a car," Dove said.

"Yeah," I agreed. "Just a car."

The tension fell from my uncle's shoulders. He laughed and held his hand out.

"Case closed, then. Good job, ghost hunters."

One by one, he dragged us on board the dinghy. We lay in the bottom, side by side by side like smelts on a drying rack. Although the day was still hot, cottony clouds had massed to the west and beyond them the sky had darkened, chain-lightning flickering like pale brass. Whippoorwills called from the shore maples and the sound stirred something in me, a lightness of body, though it was probably just the nitrogen releasing from my blood.

Uncle C lounged, eyes closed. He'd taken his shirt off and I saw the ugly scars on his chest. Each was a few inches long, arrayed in a haphazard pattern from his belly button up to his pectorals. When I'd once asked Mom how he'd gotten them, she'd said, "Just an old accident."

I cast my gaze across the water, worried for reasons I couldn't name. I spied a van idling on the shattered roadway near the eastern remains of the bridge. I could just make out Lexington Galbraith standing in front of it, with his arms crossed. I waved to him, but Lex got in his van and backed out of sight.

By now the shoreline was dotted with fishermen and families. The storm clouds had moved south towards the cursed city of Buffalo. I slumped over the side of the dinghy on my stomach. Dove did the same beside me and I felt the most thrilling thing— the pressure of our hips touching, ever so lightly.

A turtle paddled around the dinghy. Its head telescoped from its shell as it swam between our hands. Dove set her fingertip on its red-dappled head. The turtle's neck arched to feel her touch. Dove's finger trailed lightly over its shell.

We floated aimlessly, wordlessly, savouring the day.

iv.

July wore into the dog days of August. The heat fell like a guillotine blade at first light. By noon you felt as if you were breathing through boiled wool.

The kids of Cataract City took to their basements— most of them unfinished, with bare cement walls weeping moisture. We did what Canadian kids do on unbearably hot summer days: watched reruns of *The Beachcombers* and *Danger Bay* on the CBC, played endless games of Clue, Monopoly and Stratego, chucked darts at old corkboards, read *Archie* comics on sofas that had been displaced from the living room to dodder out their days as basement relics. Every so often we'd hoist ourselves up to the basement window, get a lungful of broiling late summer air and go back to our subterranean existence.

On Civic Day, the first Monday in August, Dove and I found my father's old *Playboy*s.

We didn't hang out much that summer, just the two of us, but every so often Dove would drop by unannounced and attach herself to me for a few hours. One time she went into the bathroom the minute she showed up and stayed in there half an hour. Soft weeping ebbed under the door, but when she came out she was fine. Nobody would get her to admit it, but Dove was lonely. I remember her walking up to a group of girls standing outside Paula's Elegant Bride, admiring the gowns in the window. Dove said, "If Miss Havisham had gone with that sassy taffeta number instead, hey, who knows, maybe it would've been all peaches and cream." There was something poisonous in those girls' expressions. They had no clue what she was talking about, and held their own stupidity against this stranger who'd exposed it.

One of them said, "You wear boy's shoes."

Dove looked at them, said, "They're Chuck Taylors. Good for all species."

The girl said, "There's a weird boy down my street who wears them."

"I hope the boy down the street wears your skin for Halloween," Dove told her evenly.

Thing was, I could tell Dove wanted those girls to like her. Dove wanted everyone to like her. Uncle C accepted—more than that, *embraced*—Dove exactly as she was, but he was one of the few. Living in Cataract City shrank Dove, because it asked her to be so much less. Hanging out with me must have swelled her back to her rightful size, which I guess was why every few weeks she'd stop by for a top-up.

The *Playboy*s were stashed in a cardboard box secured with packing tape. Dove found it behind the Nautilus machine my father had taken to working out with a few winters ago. We were goofing around, trying to heave up the weight stack. We had collapsed onto the bench when the box caught Dove's eye. She picked up the stack-topper. Monique St. Pierre, Miss November 1978, graced the cover. Dove paged through to the centrefold and let the fold-out flip down.

"'Turnoffs: hypocrites, phonies, litterbugs.'" Dove blew a fringe of hair off her eyes with a short, hard puff. "Deep, man."

The *Playboy*s had the feel of racy antiques. Their covers were sun-bleached and abraded with age, full of advertisements for cars that were no longer manu-factured—*Test-drive the new General Motors Corvair and drive the FUTURE!*—and obsolete products hawked by bygone pitchmen—Victor Kiam says, *I loved the Remington Electric Shaver so much, I bought the company!* Each page trumpeted the "Playboy Life-style," which involved spinning "platters," buying bubble-shaped furniture and wearing a smoking jacket in public.

There was also the ticklish matter of all the flesh

on display. Discreetly draped in mosquito netting or not, the women were still naked, so leafing through the pages with Dove made me feel weird. She seemed fascinated by the way the Playmates held their bodies, in poses suggestive of unspoken and unspecified pleasures.

"What do you think?" She leaned back on the weight bench, simpering, one leg stretched out. "This about right?"

Upstairs, I heard the front door open. Oh, God. It must be my mother, home from her holiday half-day at work.

"Jake, what did I tell you about leaving your dirty shoes in the hall?"

Dove and I were shovelling the magazines back into the box as my mother's heels hit the top step of the basement stairs. Dove slapped the flaps shut and sat on the box with her legs crossed. When Mom saw us, her chin tucked.

"Jake, you haven't introduced me to your friend."

"I'm Dove," Dove answered for herself.

"Ah, yes. Jake's told me about you."

"Only good things, I hope."

My mother eyed Dove sharply. "He told me you chew tobacco."

I cringed. "You smoke cigarettes," I reminded her.

My mother's eyes narrowed at me. But bringing up

Dove's chewing habit was dirty pool, I told myself; not to mention out of character for Mom.

"I don't chew it, Mrs. Baker, I pouch it right here." Dove pulled her bottom lip down to display her gums, then let it snap back.

"Shopkeepers shouldn't be selling you that stuff. You're far too young."

Dove winked. "I'm older than my years."

I could tell my mother didn't like that wink. "What were you two up to down here?"

"Just hanging out, Mom. We're going for a bike ride if that's okay."

My mother nodded, her head moving in a slow up-and-down like an oil derrick. "So long as you're home before dinner."

After bouncing on the box-flaps to make sure they were flattened down, Dove stood.

"Nice to meet you, Mrs. Baker."

"And you, Dove," Mom said.

Dove and I pedalled out of my subdivision. Other than us, the only things that moved were the clouds drifting across the hazy sky and the foil streamers fluttering on window-mounted A/C units. We caught the odd kid staring at us from basement windows. Their eyes were round, wondering. We slogged it through the Lion's Club park, our tires raising rooster-tails of dust that hung suspended in the air.

"My mom's working the holiday," Dove said. "The hospital's air-conditioned."

A blast of cold air met us as we walked into the emergency room of the Niagara Falls General. The waiting room was occupied by a man in a tank top with a surgical patch over his eye and another man with a goitre the size of a Brazil nut on his neck. Dove led me up a flight of stairs to the main-floor cafeteria with its steam trays of powdered eggs, then down a terrazzo-tiled hallway—we wended between patients in their hospital johnnies taking their glucose drips for a walk—to the dialysis ward on the fourth floor, where her mother worked.

Dove explained the dialysis procedure to me. "Our blood cleans itself, right? The kidneys and liver and other organs, they pull the gunk out. Like, when I chew tobacco, some of that crap gets in my blood. But my body cleans it, right? Some people, their blood doesn't do that. The gunk swims around, making them sick. So, they come here to my mom. She hooks them up to this machine that cleans it for them."

The patients in the dialysis ward were of all ages: old men and women, people my folks' age, a girl younger than me. Blood flowed up a tube in that little girl's arm, feeding into a machine the size of a dishwasher with a glass window. Her blood cycled behind the glass like red flags in a clothes dryer.

"What are you doing here, my girl?"

Dove's mother had appeared behind us. I was reminded how she had an uncanny way of popping up in your blind spot.

"What, I can't visit my mamma?"

Mrs. Yellowbird cast a withering gaze over Dove. "What did you do?"

"Nothing!"

"Is my daughter telling the truth, Jake?"

I couldn't say for sure, but nodded anyway.

Mrs. Yellowbird said, "Since you're here, you may as well make yourselves useful."

She led us to the storeroom, walking with the limp I'd noticed before. For the next hour, Dove and I stacked dialysis mixture. It looked like syrupy club soda. I asked Dove if the patients could feel the bubbles fizzing in their veins. She said no, the machines burst the bubbles before they got inside, because a bubble in your blood could be carried to your heart, get lodged in a ventricle and kill you. Once the boxes were stacked we returned to the ward, where Mrs. Yellowbird gave Dove a precise peck on the cheek. The little girl we had seen before was asleep on a cot in the day room. Dove put a cookie on a Styrofoam plate for her to eat when she woke up.

We left the hospital and biked up Valley Way. I followed Dove as she headed towards the Greyhound depot. She locked her bike to a rack and stepped through the front door. By the time I had locked my own bike and entered the station, she was consulting the out-of-town fares, which were tacked to a corkboard near the ticket wicket.

"What are you doing?"

"Blowing this pop stand."

She pulled a crumpled wad of bills from her pocket. "Cashed in my salamander stash yesterday. Those bastards at Pick of the Critter lowballed me—five bucks a head, when they promised ten—but hey, bygones."

Dove had about fifty dollars. She seemed deathly serious about hopping a Greyhound.

"Where are you going?"

"Away."

"Away where?"

She chucked her chin at the corkboard. "Plenty of options."

"Why?"

"It's time."

Twenty minutes ago, her mother had given her a kiss. A goodbye kiss, sure, but not *Goodbye forever, daughter of mine, and may the road ease your troubled mind.*

Dove stepped up to the wicket. "I need a ticket. One-way."

I wanted to grab her arm, the way you'd do with

someone perched at the edge of a cliff. I prayed the guy behind the glass would say it was illegal for a fourteen-year-old to board a bus without supervision, but he only stared through the grey corona of cigarette smoke enrobing his head.

"You don't have clothes or a toothbrush or anything," I said to Dove. "Shouldn't you tell someone? Your mom or—"

"They'd just try to stop me, duh." She addressed the guy. "How far can twenty-five bucks take me, one-way?"

The guy sucked on his cigarette. "East, west, south, north?"

"Wherever the action is."

"Twenty-one'll get you to Windsor."

"When's it leave?"

"Five minutes."

Snatching my elbow in a pincer grip, Dove marched me over to the corner of the station. We stood next to a vending machine whose coils hung empty apart from the bottom-tier items: Eat-More, Big Turk, some cinnamon-flavoured toothpicks.

"You think I'm crazy, don't you?"

"No."

"Sure you do. You think I'm looney-tunes."

"No."

"I'm crackers. Cuckoo for Cocoa Puffs. Spun, screwball, crazypants—"

"I think you're like the sun."

Dove bent forward as if she'd been stabbed in the stomach. She quickly straightened, but not before I saw the strange wound I'd delivered, the pained twist to her lips.

"Who told you to say that?"

"Nobody. I just—it was my own—"

"You're lying." Dove said so with a sigh, as if she'd already forgiven me. She slung her arm over my shoulder.

"It's okay. Could be I am a bit crazy. The possibility's crossed my mind. But I don't want to hurt anyone. I just want to do what I do."

In that moment, her desire made sense to me because with her arm around my shoulder, the insistent squeeze of her fingers, she *made* it make sense.

"Don't try to save me, Jake. You'll just let yourself down."

Half an hour ago we'd been stacking dialysis mix and now she was hopping on a bus and lighting out for parts unknown. The whiplash effect made me sick.

"I'm going to tell someone, Dove."

"Okay. Maybe that's why I brought you here."

She walked back to the wicket. When she saw I hadn't budged, she flicked her hand: *Shoo, fly.* I slunk outside. A bus was queued in the corral. People were stashing suitcases in the luggage compartment. I unlocked my bike and pedalled down to the pay phone outside Mac's Milk. Unlacing one shoe, I peeled my tube sock off and shook out the sixty-five cents stuck to the pad of my foot. I deposited a quarter in the slot and dialed the Yellowbird house. The answering machine picked up.

"This is Jake . . . uh, Jake Baker? I wanted to tell you that Dove, she's at the, at the bus station? Not a city bus. To another city. Maybe you told her that was, uh, okay or something?"

I kept the phone pressed to my ear in the hope that Billy would pick up, until the machine made a *beeeep*. When I returned to the depot, both the bus and Dove were gone.

V.

The sun had begun to sink behind the trees by the time I got home. I caught my mother and father in the midst of a blistering argument.

"I read the articles," my dad was saying as I stepped through the door. "Vladimir Nabokov has published stories in *Playboy*."

"Yeah, the second-rate ones he couldn't convince the *New Yorker* to publish."

"It was an intellectual magazine, once upon a time. Tasteful nudes, yes? You could put the magazine on your coffee table."

"At what venue?" my mother wanted to know. "A car-key party at a swingers' pad?" Her anger was shot through with genuine hurt. "Why would you keep those things around?"

"They're no different than my old bowling trophies. They're just *there*."

"Were you still buying them when we started . . . ?"

"Go check the dates, Cece. You won't find a single issue once we started going steady. I figured they were valuable. Collectibles, y'know?"

"Were you planning to leave them in our will? Jake's inheritance?"

Seizing his opportunity, my father made a wild stab at levity. "I was, but our son screwed it up." He jabbed his finger at me: "You're out of the will, Jake. No more *Playboy*s. I'll donate them to science, same as my organs."

Mom rolled her eyes. "What would science need with your *Playboy*s?"

"I haven't the foggiest," Dad said magnanimously, "but science is welcome to them. Grind them up to pulp and create a cure for some grave ill."

"How about a cure for terminal boyhood," my mother suggested.

One fire doused, at least partially, my father wheeled on me. "And what the hell are you doing poking around in boxes that don't concern you?"

"Don't blame him, Sam. He was just doing what a boy does. Besides which, I'm not sure it was his idea. Our son had a girl in the house today."

A flush crawled up my neck. "Did Billy call?"

Mom tapped her watch. "He did not. You're late, too. I said before suppertime."

"I'm sorry. I just—"

"You're grounded for a week."

Mom hadn't grounded me in years. And this sentence felt particularly unfair, seeing as I'd spent but a small and pointless fraction of the day looking at smutty old magazines. The lion's share had passed at the Greyhound station, with me in a state of dread.

My father said, "You don't think that's a tad harsh?"

She shot him a you-stay-out-of-this look, but he wasn't to be cowed.

"You can't force the kid into isolation. Lord knows he manages that pretty well on his own. He's found some friends. Why take that away?"

"I'm not taking anything away. I'm punishing him. Fairly."

"Ahhh, Cece, come on . . ."

My father's "come on" wasn't a plea for leniency. Rather, his tone indicated that my mother was hiding her true reasoning, maybe even from herself. "You can't bubble-wrap him," he added.

"Is that what you think I'm doing?"

"Head to your room, sport," Dad said to me. "Your mom and I ought to talk."

The events of the past hours had left me too confused and defeated to protest, so I slouched upstairs. My folks' discussion lasted nearly an hour. I recall one thing my father said, his voice rolling up the staircase.

"Our boy owes us nothing. No boy owes his parents. Parents owe their children everything, always and unconditionally, and that's just the way it goes."

Afterwards my mother knocked on my bedroom door and sat on the bed beside me. "You're grounded for two days." Her weary exhalation said that while the punishment might be silly, rules were rules. She kissed me on the forehead and again on the lips.

"I only want you to be happy, Jake. But first I want you to be safe."

I pictured Mrs. Yellowbird speaking those same words to Dove, sitting on her daughter's bed. I didn't know it then, but I'd speak those same words to my own son one day.

"Okay, Mom."

"I love you."

"Love you, too."

And I did. Just not quite as much as she loved me.

5.

THE HOUSE ON THE HILL

Exactly twenty-three years after Dove hopped on the Greyhound, my son was born at St. Joseph's Hospital in the west end of Toronto. He was delivered on Civic Day, via emergency C-section. The umbilical cord was wrapped around his belly, trapping him inside my wife's womb like a dog on a leash. His heartbeat began to fail, but I had no idea. The monitors were so different from the ones in my own surgical theatre. The duty nurses confabbed, and next thing I knew, a pair of orderlies were spiriting my wife from the room, rolling her bed away—"What's happening?" I kept asking, but nobody seemed interested in telling me.

My wife called out to me as the orderlies wheeled her from the room. I pursued her down the hall to the OR, where her obstetrician stopped me with a literal stiff arm to the chest.

"Wait out here," she said.

"I'm a surgeon, too. Brains. Over to St. Mike's," I said, replacing *at* with *to* in true Cataract City fashion—when flustered, I found myself resorting to old verbal tics.

"And I'm sure you're a dab hand at brains."

She rucked up her sleeves and squirted carbolic soap onto her hands, working it into a lather at the washbasin. It smelled the same as the stuff at St. Mike's—cherry, like the sticks of brittle gum that came inside old packs of baseball cards. Like Dove's chewing tobacco.

"Wait here," she said. "The nurse will come get you."

"Just . . . do no harm, okay?"

"No need to quote the scripture at me, doctor."

I paced the hallway like a caged bear. The day before, everything had been normal—boring, even. It's hard to comprehend how fantastic normality can be until . . . a nurse came out. She handed me a hairnet and a pair of sterile booties to slip over my shoes.

Past the swinging doors, the obstetrician's eyes were the colour of shaved ice above her face mask. I sat in a chair near my wife's head. A sheet hung vertically to shield her stomach. The obstetrician worked behind it. My wife's eyes were huge and round, the pupils blown out from the meds. I didn't know where to look—it was so much easier to wield the blade.

At some point our son started to cough, then scream. It was the best sound I'd ever heard. When the nurse handed him to me, I felt disoriented—my son had a banana-head, back-sloped and elongated, an infant as dreamt by H.R. Giger. I reminded myself that this was normal: the plates of a baby's skull are extremely flexible to aid their passage through the birth canal. Within days my son's head would look as it should.

They gave our son to me—not to my wife, who had carried and nourished him. Because of the method of delivery, she couldn't be the first to touch him, so I kissed her and told her how sorry I was for that.

The nurse wrapped our son in a towel and ushered me into the hallway. My boy's pupils were massive, his irises delineated by the thinnest band of blue. His mouth kept opening and closing. His lips made a wet *pok*. There was something disturbingly mindless to this sight. Eyes that didn't appear to chart anything, the mouth opening and closing like a fish as it suffocated on the deck of a trawler. It reminded me, too, of the look of a patient whose brain had "coned." Before those patients pass on, a look overtakes their faces. It doesn't matter how heavily they may be sedated, the look is the same. Was my minutes-old son giving me that look?

A new breed of fear crept into my heart, different from anything I'd ever felt. Maybe this was just how freshly born humans behaved. I knew brains, not babies. But maybe . . . had he been inside my wife too long? Had he opened his mouth to take his first real breath and inhaled amniotic fluid? Had his brain—his fragile, still-quickening brain—no. *No.* It couldn't be. I said this to myself even though I knew by then that, oh my, yes, unfair things did happen. All the time they happened, every minute of every day, to people good and bad alike.

In the hallway of a hospital two hundred miles from my childhood home, I stood cradling the most precious object I would ever hold—a child I already loved more than he would ever be capable of loving me back—as scared as I'd ever been. It wasn't the fear I'd known as a boy: that onrushing smash-cut terror of a monster leaping from a closet. This was the gnawing fear of possibility, the creeping fear of consequence.

Don't do this. I remember this plea, though I cannot

say who or what I was sending it out to. *Not to our baby boy. Do it to me. Hurt* me, *wreck* me, *take every-thing from* me.

And all the time, I knew the world is resistant to bargains of that nature.

i

Three days after hopping a bus to parts unknown, Dove showed up at my house after dinner to ask if I wanted to light off fireworks at the scrapyard.

Billy was with her. I hadn't seen either of them since that afternoon with Dove at the bus station, though both acted as if that was only a matter of our schedules failing to line up. It felt as though the events at the Greyhound depot could forever exist in a sour bubble between us—and so long as none of us pierced its membrane, the Yellowbirds seemed content to pretend it had never happened.

Years later, Billy would tell me that his sister had taken that Greyhound to Windsor. She arrived in the evening and paid two bucks for a ticket to an all-ages punk show a half-block from the bus terminal. When the show let out in the wee hours, she walked to the 24-hour Coffee Time with some of the musicians and hangers-on. She rebuffed the bass player's invitation to head back to his place. When the others left, she bought a bag of day-old donuts. She had eaten six by the time Billy and his mother found her. As soon as the Greyhound agent had confirmed he'd sold a ticket to a girl matching Dove's description, the two of them had hit the road.

The drive home unfolded in stressed silences, broken by Dove offering her day-olds. *Try the cruller, Mom. You love crullers.* Billy confessed that the most painful part for him was hearing his mother addressing his sister in a tone of defeated bewilderment.

I can't live under your skin, Dove, baby. Can't make you stop doing these things.

That evening, she and Billy came over on their bikes. A plastic bag hung from Dove's handlebars. She showed me its contents with a conspiratorial wink. "They'll all go bang, Jake."

There were packs of Black Cats with braided fuses, Screaming Devils like sugar cones wrapped in shiny paper, a half-dozen Roman candles bundled like sticks of dynamite and some others, bright red and waxy with Chinese lettering.

"How'd you get them?"

Dove shrugged, as if to say *I know people.*

I hesitated. I wanted to tell her and Billy that, yes, I'd go with them, but I still felt weird—as if there ought to be some kind of resolution to what had gone down at the bus station.

"More for us, then," said Dove, interpreting my silence and looping the bag back over her handlebars.

"No, wait. I—I'll talk to my mom. Wait down the block, okay?"

"Why, you embarrassed to be seen with us?"

"We'll wait past the street sign," Billy said. "Come on, Dove."

I ducked inside to ask my mother if I could go bike-riding with Billy. She agreed, as long as I promised to come home in a couple of hours, before it got too dark. I met Billy and Dove at the top of the street. Fleer hockey cards were clothespinned between their bicycle spokes and as the three of us rode into the ashen evening, those cards made a Tommy-gun drone.

The Marine Salvage and Metals scrapyard was a mile west of the rail yards, nestled between towering stands of fir. The trees shadowed a yard filled with junked cars, boats and home appliances. On week-ends, folks were free to pick down the rows—a "tourist pass" cost fifty cents, payable to Chester Broomfield, the head scrap man. Everything was for sale: engines, fenders, hubcaps, antennas, even the contents of gloveboxes. All items were assessed by Chester, who assigned an ambiguous value ("Saaaaaaay, two bucks?"), opening the door to haggling. But Chester's prices were so rock-bottom that people rarely bothered to barter.

Chester also operated the auto-crusher. Called either Cube-A-Saurus Rex or the Squashinator by local kids, the pneumatic brute was capable of reducing two tons of Detroit rolling iron to the size of a packing box. According to Uncle C, the corpses of Cataract City's underbelly-dwellers sometimes wound up in those cars before being sent to the smelter.

The perfect disposal, my uncle claimed. *Although tossing them over the falls is another fail-safe: a human body gets so waterlogged, pounded by a million tons of water, that the flesh becomes soggy as wet newspaper and flakes away for the fish to eat.*

After losing his right leg to diabetes, Chester had lapsed into a state of semi-retirement. He was still around on the weekends to dicker with anyone who'd consent to it, but on weekdays he was gone and his replacement, the charmless Doug Rowe—brother of Stanley—worked light hours.

In Chester's absence, the scrapyard had become a kid's paradise. Children spent their days behind the wheels of cars playing cops and robbers, or captaining the old catamarans and motorboats propped up on cinder blocks. And this was where the *Playboy* lifestyle had gone to die. *Drive the FUTURE—straight to the junkyard!*

We propped our bikes against a stack of rotting rail ties and found a spot in the fence where the chain-link had been snipped. Billy peeled back a flap so we could squirm through into the yard. Wind scraped over the hulks of old DeSotos and Pintos, filling my nose with the tang of rust. Some kids might have been hiding in the outlying slag heaps or playing tag over by Cube-A-Saurus Rex, but to us, the place felt deserted.

We walked down a row of flattened cars piled atop one another like playing cards. Their flattened carcasses rose fifteen feet up, and squeaks emanated from within: the cars made great shelter for animals—and with the scrapyard being so close to the train yards, it wasn't unusual for rail bums to crash here, too.

The Salvage was set up like the spokes on a wheel: every row funnelled to the central hub where Chester's shack had once sat. Now there was only a bare circle of earth dotted with snatches of duckweed and knots of purple flowers that seemed tragically out of place.

When we reached the hub, Dove dropped the sack of fireworks and produced a tarnished Zippo from the pocket of her cut-offs. She spun the flywheel until a spark caught the wick.

"Ignition, check," she said, snapping the lighter shut with a deft flick of her wrist.

We sat on the buckled hood of an ancient Jeep Willy as the sky paled above the treetops. The quality of light in our part of the world was such that, just before night fell, the horizon lit up with an almost other-worldly glow. I never discovered why that was . . . probably the final rays of sunlight reflecting off the river basin caused this fleeting incandescence. But as a kid I thought it must be because the sun itself— that unfeeling ball of gas—didn't want to leave, and so it lingered, clawing up the ragged hub of the earth in order to shed the last of its light over us.

Billy drummed his kneecaps with two Roman Candles: *dappa-dappa-dap-dap-da-dap*. We didn't speak much. It was good to be out, the three of us, on a late-summer night.

"Yessir," came a voice, "if I was a kid lookin' to stir up some shit, this is just the spot I'd mosey to."

The owner of that voice unfolded himself from the front seat of a crumpled Dodge thirty feet away. The gathering shadows clung to his body as his limbs unfurled from the wreck with spidery grace.

"Firecrackers, uh? Goddamn, you'll have your-selves a time."

The man was tall—taller than Uncle C, even—and much thicker than my uncle. His hair was twisted into ropes, and a steel-wool beard draped his face. He wore track pants, a sleeveless coat smeared with grease, and engineer's boots with metal winking at the toes. The track pants were most disturbing: my gym teacher, Mr. O'Meara, wore the same ones—but his were always clean, whereas this guy's were streaked with slashes of what might be dark paint.

He advanced towards us with a darting stride. From his looks, I had expected him to shamble, but the guy could motor. Billy slid off the Jeep's hood.

"We'll go someplace else," Dove said.

"No, no. Stay. Let's light them puppies up."

When the man smiled, it did something to his face, sharpened the angles.

"You don't figure I'll call the cops on you, do ya?" he said. "Me 'n' the pigs have seen enough of each other to last a hundred lifetimes."

The man shoved his hands into his pockets. They moved around under the fabric. It reminded me of a kid in my class, Brodie Gregg, who stood by the monkey bars at recess doing the same thing while staring moony-eyed into space. The girls nicknamed Brodie "Pocket Pool."

Dove shifted to her left—and the man shifted with her, shadowing her. It was a little thing, but a lot seemed to hang on that sidling movement. The man's smile persisted but there was definitely something hostile to it now. Dove spat a stream of tobacco juice into the weeds and watched him.

"You're a dipper, huh?" the guy said.

Dove was smiling a little now, too. "You want some?" She flipped him the puck.

The man yanked his hands out of his pockets quick enough to catch it. He pinched a big wad and packed it behind his chalky, cracked lips. Shreds of tobacco bristled above his lip like hair sprouting from a lounge lizard's shirt collar. He tucked the puck into his pocket as if it was his now.

"I'll get you back in trade," he told Dove. "I *insist*."

I became aware of how the scrapyard floated in a cocoon of isolation, well past the main roads. You could scream until your lungs ruptured and the sound might not touch a single pair of human ears. I cut a glance at the Yellowbirds. A vein pulsed softly in Dove's throat, while Billy's face held a pale intensity. Their bodies were near-motionless, like twin icebergs at sea.

"Light them up," the man said, gesturing again at the firecrackers. "Or is there some other game you'd rather play?"

A languid, blissed-out look spread across his face. The machinery of society, with its laws and lawmen, was grinding away elsewhere—and he was crouched in its blind spot.

"Where do you come from?" Billy asked.

"Why do you want to know, son?"

"Haven't seen you around."

The man's hands balled into fists. They were re-markably clean and unscarred considering their owner slept in junked cars. I noticed his face bore no scars, either—beneath his patchy beard lurked a fussy, boarding-school softness.

When it seemed like the man was gathering himself to make a move at Billy, Dove said, "You like to play games?"

Her hand slipped up under her shirt, pulling up the hem to give a flash of bare flat tummy. The man's hands returned to his pockets. He rocked from side to side as if he had to urinate.

"You're a tiger, aren't ya? Look at that, now . . ."

His eyes were riveted on that slash of bare stom-ach. He unzipped his jacket and rubbed his own stomach through his dirty T-shirt. Dove smiled, but it was an empty grin, as if an essential part of her had retreated into a sheltered spot in her subcon-scious, while a strange girl had stepped in to take her place. Whatever game she and the guy were play-ing, it occurred at some dog-whistle frequency I was unable to comprehend.

She flicked the Zippo, spun the flywheel. The flame popped alight.

The man said, "The little girl who liked to play with fire."

He approached her with a peculiar motion. I couldn't see his feet moving and yet he drew nearer without seeming to, like a snake slithering.

Dove held out one hand, her index finger ticking like a metronome. *Uh-uh, no you don't.*

The man gave a sickly smile, pausing to enjoy the show. Dove's other hand, the one holding the lit Zippo, flirted down one leg of her cut-offs and up the other. The man's gaze followed the flame as it tracked over Dove's body. Its fire scorched the frayed threads at the bottom of her shorts, raising plumes of smoke. She tossed the still-lit Zippo on the ground a few feet from me, and near Billy's sneakers. The man's eyes darted to it before returning to Dove, riveted on her tick-ticking finger, the hypnotic sway of her hips.

Maybe he failed to see the Roman candle in Billy's hand, or maybe he didn't care. Did he even hear the fizzle as Billy touched its wick to the flame? To judge from his shocked look when Billy brought the firework up and pointed it squarely at his face, he had not.

"The hell?"

For a nerve-shattering instant I thought the fire-work was a dud. The man would slap it out of Billy's hand and set about whatever viciousness he'd been casually delaying. . . .

Then a flaming ball shot from the paper tube and hit the man in his face.

The bloodied light bloomed before the man's eyes and he reeled backwards, clawing at his face. The firework had struck above his lips. The phosphorus singed a great deal of his beard off and left a soot mark on his nose, which looked black as a rotted potato. He went down on his ass, jerking backwards like a fiddler crab. Pressing his palms to his eye sockets, he screeched: "I'm blind! Oh, Jesus Christ Jesus mercy—!"

Dove grabbed the firework as another ball leapt from the tube and struck the man's chest. She took a darting step forward and crammed the Roman candle down the guy's shirt. The next ball—bright blue— shot straight down. His shirt blew outwards like the wind filling a boat sail. I could see the shape of his body lit in electric blue, like an X-ray.

Dove wheeled on us and said, "Move your asses already!"

The three of us tore down the closest row of scrapped cars, shoes pelting the dirt, adrenalin redlined. This, I knew, was different than running from a school-yard bully like Terry Vreeland. The worst Terry would ever do was put your arm in a chicken-wing or deliver a few skull-ringing rabbit punches. If the bearded stranger caught us, there was no telling what he'd do.

I'll never forget the fear-fed momentum I felt running through that moonlit scrapyard. I swear my body expanded under my skin, an on-the-fly growth spurt born of sheer necessity, as if my pituitary gland had said, *The kid needs it NOW!*

Billy cut around the row at the yard's edge. "Oh no."

We'd run down the wrong path. The rip in the fence wasn't there. Our bikes weren't there. Somewhere in the depths of the yard there arose a glittering howl.

Billy flicked his head, instructing Dove and me to follow. We slunk over two rows, ducked like soldiers in a trench, skirted a stack of cars and crouched lower. It was hard to hear anything over the sound of my own tortured breathing. I willed myself to inhale deeply—deep but *ooooh* so quiet—to calm the drumming of my heart.

Billy poked his head around a bumper and scanned the fence. He ducked back and pointed up the row. Dove and I dogged his heels without making much noise on the gravel. I willed my footsteps to be light and as nimble as a fox, not to crunch the dead weeds or step on jags of metal.

The row emptied back into the central hub. We broke into a crouched run around Cube-A-Saurus Rex. My tongue felt coated in dust. We clustered, shoulder to shoulder, our eyes ticking over the yard. . . .

The scrapyard lights *thunked* on. They were the same kind you find at the baseball diamond: sodium vapour lamps set atop metal stalks. Were they set on timers to switch on at dusk? If not, this meant the man must have found the control box and switched them on.

Squinting across the yard, I tried to find the row we'd come down, the row that led back to our bikes, to escape, but they all looked the same—

The man heaved into view fifty yards away. Except he didn't look like a man at all now. He had become a Beast: an enraged half-burnt *thing*, the sort you'd see crawling out of a grave as maggots pitter-pattered from its eye sockets. Charred holes were smoked through its shirt and it moved with a twisted-ankle limp. A ragged ring of soot occupied the middle of its face and it was clutching a tire iron.

The feral eyes of the Beast locked with my own as it began to shamble towards us.

"*Go!*" Dove hissed.

We raced down one row and fled back up another. Through a gap in the cars I saw the Beast stomping down the row we'd vacated. When Billy made it to the head of the row, he did something that struck me as either daring or suicidal: he went *back down* the row the Beast had only just left, doubling back on our own footsteps. He hazarded a glance at his sister, nodded, then scrambled under the nearest car.

Dove grabbed my elbow so fiercely that she could have pulled it out of its joint, though at the time I barely felt a thing. She dragged me under a car on the opposite side of the row. We lay flat on our stomachs, staring across at Billy. My breath puffed up clouds of dust. Black dots popped before my eyes. I thought I'd faint—then I caught Dove staring at me with a flinty intensity that said: *If you faint I won't be able to help you, so don't.*

Gravel crunched under the Beast's heels as it approached. I heard a grinding sound: the tire iron dragging over the dirt. The Beast's boots entered my sightline. My body went rigid and my lungs locked up. The Beast inhaled as if it was smelling the air, trying to locate our scent. It spoke to itself, in a blistered rasp. "You sewered me. Now I'm gonna sewer you."

It snarled, bashing the tire iron against the car we lay under. My heart seized as flakes of rust rained down.

"Nobody's here," the Beast muttered to itself. "Do it. You'll like it. *Do* it. It's easy. Do it and hop the next freight out of town . . . go for it. *Do it.*"

The Beast continued down the row. I heard it break into a trot, then a run, then the scrape of its boots blended with the other furtive sounds of night.

We waited, flattened to the ground. At last, Dove wiggled out from under the car. She crept forward on her toes and fingertips, hunched in the middle of the row, scanned both ways and waved us out. Billy joined her, but I couldn't. My fingers clawed into the dirt and my limbs were paralyzed.

The Yellowbirds looked at me beseechingly. Billy held his hand out and mouthed, "*Please, Jake.*"

Taking his hand, I was able to squirm out. We crept down the row to the yard's edge, where I spied the rip in the fence. Had I ever seen a more beautiful sight than our bikes canted carelessly against those rail ties? We slipped through the rip, hopped on our bikes and fled, standing high in the saddle as our legs churned the pedals, not daring to sit down until we'd reached the outer suburbs.

We reached my street slicked in sweat. I couldn't shake the possibility that the Beast had followed us. I pictured it lumbering out of the shadows, past the street lamps, its tire iron kicking up sparks on the pavement.

"Come to my house?" I asked the Yellowbirds. "My dad can drive you home."

"Nah," Dove said with a casual wave of her hand.

I parked my bike in the garage and snuck past Mom and Dad, who were watching *St. Elsewhere.* I slipped upstairs and collapsed into bed. Then I got up and made sure the window was locked. I stunk of sweat and fireworks. I peeled off my shirt, wadded it up and swabbed my armpits before burying it at the bottom of the clothes hamper.

I never told my parents what happened that night. Now I wonder: How often must that occur? A boy comes within an ace of death or disappearance, then returns home and goes to sleep and his parents never suspect a thing.

I closed my eyes and thought about how serene the Yellowbirds had been. Then I thought of how their mother walked with that limp, which forced me to consider the fact that their father wasn't in the picture. Dove and Billy had never brought him up, not once.

A thought flashed through my mind. Could their father have been the one who'd given their mother that limp? Had there been nights when he'd thundered through the house like a storm, raining down blows on his wife and children? Nights when only Billy and Dove's wits and resilience had prevented him from laying lifelong marks upon their bodies? Was that what had instilled in them the calm I'd seen in the scrapyard?

In fact, I now know this to be true, at least partially. Years later, I would talk with Billy in the dorm room we shared as freshmen, and he would tell me that yes, his father had been a monster, but that it was his *father's* father, Billy's grandfather on his father's side, who had clouted his mother with a length of stove wood and crushed her kneecap. The only way Billy's mother could ensure the poison didn't leach into her own children's lives was to get away. . . . Billy had sat on his dorm-room cot with his "I Want to Believe" poster tacked to the wall and told me all this without flinching, his voice calm and measured, though his hands were shaking just a bit.

As a boy, when I'd looked at the houses down my block, and all over Cataract City, I'd believed that the lives unfurling behind those doors were much the same as my own. Every boy and girl had good parents like my parents. Every child went to bed with a full belly, in a warm bed, knowing they were loved. That was the life every child was supposed to have, wasn't it?

I slipped into sleep thinking about Mrs. Yellowbird's limp, which I decided she must have earned confronting a ticked-off wolverine back in Slave Lake. She'd fought that threat, sacrificing herself to protect her children.

As this was the most comforting possibility, my young mind embraced it as fact.

ii.

The second-to-last meeting of the Saturday Night Ghost Club—and, as it turned out, the last one Billy would attend—found us standing inside the whistling black skeleton of a house that had burnt to cinders before I was born. The usual suspects were present: Uncle C, Billy, myself and, somewhat reluctantly, Lexington Galbraith.

My uncle had proposed the foray a few days prior at So Beta! Billy and I had been browsing the empty aisles—Billy had his eyes on a copy of *Butcher, Baker, Nightmare Maker*—while Lex ate jujubes behind the counter, all except the red ones. It was around then that a woman stalked into the shop.

"Where is she?"

Lex feigned nonchalance. "Where is who, Jan, my dear?"

I peeked over the rack with fresh interest. This must be Janet Templeton, Lex's ex.

"You damn well know who. Becca. I thought she'd run away!"

"How can you be sure she hasn't?" Lex wanted to know.

"Because your next-door neighbour Edna Simms told me she'd seen Becca on your landing. Of all the sneak-thieving, low, skunky-ass things to do—"

"Hold on a sec, pump your brakes." Lex balanced an elbow on the counter, index finger pointing at Janet. "Who's the one who stole her in the first place?"

Janet slapped Lex's finger away. "When I left, you said I could take anything I wanted."

"I meant anything *inanimate*. Books. Cassette tapes. Not my only source of joy in this godforsaken world."

"How'd you get her?"

Lex's eyes flicked to us.

"For God's sake, Lexington. Isn't there something better you could be doing with your life besides coercing boys into kidnapping cats?"

"He didn't coerce us," Billy said. "He paid us."

Before Janet could react to this fresh outrage, Lex said, "*Everybody* could be doing something better with their lives, Jan. Name me one person who is doing the best, most righteous thing with their life right this very minute."

Janet uttered an inarticulate sound of disgust and stalked back out of the shop, pausing only to kick over a life-size cutout of Han Solo as she went.

Upon her departure, Lex turned wistful. "That's one hell of a lady walking out that door."

Moments later Uncle C breezed in. I hadn't seen him much during the dog days, as his shop had been closed whenever I dropped by. I would peer through the glass window into the murky innards of the

Occultorium, and sometimes, through lifting motes of dust, I thought I spotted something hovering by the counter. A pair of wet glimmers watching me out on the sunlit safety of the street.

"I've picked the spot for our next expedition, boys," my uncle announced.

I'd never heard of the place Uncle C described to us. But had I been watching Lex, I would have wondered about the apprehension that flitted across his face.

Lex. My uncle's oldest friend. After it was all over, I would wonder why he hadn't said anything. Why didn't he tell my mother: *Cecilia, I'm worried it's starting again*? It was only much later that I understood. Unable to stop the momentum, Lex treated what was happening as an unavoidable collision: if he steered into the crash with Calvin, maybe they would both be flung harmlessly aside. And if things were predestined for ruin, well, at least my uncle would hit terminal velocity with an old friend at his side. Lex was wrong in almost all of this, but I could sympathize: my job has shown me that is what people do when those they care for are suffering.

The following Saturday evening I rode my bike to the Yellowbird home.

It was just past seven o'clock but the sky was shading a melancholy blue, as it did towards the end of the summer. The Mister Turtle pool sat at the curb with some sacks of trash. It made me think of Dove, whom I hadn't seen since that night at the junkyard.

Billy waited in his yard. We rode down Whirlpool Road past the strip clubs striped in garish neon and the no-tell motels advertising hourly rates, turning down a corduroy road edging the Niagara Parks golf course. The corduroy road devolved into a trail skirting the hydroelectric reservoir. Wind scalloped the water, bringing with it the ozone tang of electricity. The station's twin Tesla coils spiked skyward against the horizon. Blue sparks zipped between them, the sound of the electrical discharge riding the twilight to my ears: *zzzzwip! zzzzwip!*

"Philadelphia Experiment, man," Billy said with a nod at the Teslas.

Soon, an incinerated house came into view at the crest of a wind-scrubbed hill, just as Uncle C had described. All that was left of it were support beams partially burnt in the blaze, which poked towards the sky like tusks. We pedalled up lazy switchbacks to reach the crest of the hill. The reservoir was to the west, the Niagara River's limestone basin to the east, the spume from the falls visible amidst the eighty-dollar-a-night hotels to the south.

Lex's van appeared around a pine-shielded bend and rumbled up a weedy strip that, at some long-ago time, must have been a driveway. He hopped out and asked, "Your uncle here?"

No sooner had Lex said this than Uncle C appeared at the base of the hill. He stopped, striking a pensive pose in the pooling shadows. I saw him rub his forehead but he was too distant, the light too pallid, to make out his face.

When Uncle C reached us, he gave Lex a wan smile. "Ready for some ghost hunting?"

He mounted the heat-cracked steps to what had once been the front door. I could see that it had been a small home, probably perfect for a young family. The fire had consumed most of the timber and blackened the brickwork. Situated on the hill with no shelter from the wind and no hydrants for firefighters to tap, it had likely burnt fast. There was no smell of smoke anymore. No smell at all. Only a haunting sterility that made me think of how a moon rock might smell—dusty and lunar. Even dead things here on Earth have a smell: the putrid scent of their own decomposition. But this place—the inner sanctum of the old house, which we now entered—had a non-smell, something that registered to the nose the same way TV static registers to our eyes. I'd never thought that an absence of smell could be dreadful, but now I realized that yes, it could—when your senses encounter that kind of strangeness, something deep in your lizard brain pings a warning.

Danger, Will Robinson—!

"Keep your feet on the supports," my uncle cautioned. "Just picture walking on a balance beam."

We followed him across what may once have been a front room or kitchen. The beam made carbon-like fracturing noises under my high-tops.

"Cal, don't you think we ought to—"

"It's fine, Lex," my uncle tutted. "There's enough solid wood to support us."

We walked to the other side of the house, steering around what were once the basement steps, now only a steep drop into the shadows. My uncle sat on the foundation wall with his stork-like legs dangling into the weeds.

"What happened?" I asked.

"Everything I know is third-hand, fourth-hand," Uncle C admitted. "Forgive me, but . . . it happened a long time ago. A man and a woman lived here. A young couple, just married, very much in love. The man bought this whole hillside, annexed from the city, and had this house built. He figured a house way up on the hill, overlooking the water, far from the hurly-burly . . . solitude. A good place to raise a child, which was something both he and his wife must have sought."

A howl kicked up from the woods, a lonely note that ascended through several octaves before joining the low purr of the wind. My uncle had once warned me that a pack of wolves roamed outside the city limits, seven or eight timber wolves who feasted on stray dogs and cats and the deer who made their home on the escarpment. *It's the strangest thing,* he'd told me. *You will only hear them howling on nights when the moon is full. Must be a coincidence, hmm?*

"It happened at night," Uncle C continued. "A night like this or any other, except in winter. The couple had recently moved in. There were stacks of boxes everywhere, breakables wrapped in newspaper. The edge of night moved in, dropping fast as it does in winter. Out of that frigid darkness, men came. No one knows who they were, or where they came from. Drifters or criminals or just men who'd come together over a mutual joy in terrorizing the weaker of our species. They must have spied the house atop the hill and known, instinctively, that this was where to go."

Uncle C drew in a breath, as if to orient himself on some detail buried within the folds of his memory.

Gently, Lex said, "We're right here with you, Cal. Isn't that right, boys?"

My uncle smiled gratefully. "One man knocked on the door. The smallest of them, the rattiest and least threatening probably. He'd got lost in the woods, he claimed. The couple were deceived by his wretchedness and invited him in, never imagining . . . it's like with vampires, boys. Once you invite them over the threshold, you're theirs. The rat-faced man didn't even take his boots off. He walked into the kitchen tracking mud over the floor and basked in the heat from the wood stove. After looking this way and that to make sure nobody else was at home, he took a knife off the cutting board—the woman had been cutting potatoes for dinner—and sawed through the phone cord. It was then, I'm sure, that the couple got an inkling of the hell they'd invited into their home. Rat-face slunk to the sink and softly, with just the tip of the knife, tapped on the window. *Tap, tap, tap, tap*—little pig, little pig, let me in . . .

"The fact, boys, is that ninety-nine percent of violent encounters are decided within the first moments. You have a few precious seconds to understand the threat and make a choice. Your attackers leverage that indecision against you. You believe that maybe, if you do as they say, they might just . . . go away. People think home invasions happen in other places, to other unlucky people, not us—even *while* these events are unfolding.

"Some other men came in. They filed into the kitchen one after the other, their bodies unkinking from the cold. Can you imagine it? You open your front door and invite death inside."

My uncle's description was so matter-of-fact I couldn't help but see it vividly. The house locked in a wintry isolation. The vantage in my mind's eye was omniscient, hovering someplace over the reservoir. Squares of light burnt in the windows—and fleetingly, frighteningly, I saw movement. Dark shapes gliding behind the glass.

"There is no record of what those men did that night," my uncle continued briskly. "That's the only merciful part of this story. After they'd done what they'd done, they left."

Billy said, "They didn't burn the house?"

"They left it intact except for the two people inside. The men disappeared back into the darkness. None of them were ever found or brought to justice."

My uncle's flat, unfeeling tone only made this fact more terrifying: that there could be men like that out there, circling the burning fires of civilization, waiting for us to step away from the light.

"The man and woman were still alive. Why they'd been left that way was and is another mystery. But the woman was badly hurt. Bleeding and . . . and other things. The man waited as long as he could—he wanted to make sure the men were gone—before carrying his wife to the car. The battery wires had been cut, but the man knew how to fix them. Still, it took time. He stood in the cold, his numb and blood-oiled hands frantically braiding the wires while his wife lay in the car, getting colder and colder."

Lex made a small movement, and I wondered if he would protest that the story was too much for me and Billy. But he only braced his palms on his knees, as if to stem some deep internal pain.

"He got the car started," my uncle went on, "and down the little laneway right there, I guess"—he pointed vaguely—"and out to the road, which would have been narrower back then, unlit by street lamps. He drove as fast as he could. Faster than was safe. He got into town, and to the hospital, but it was too late."

"She died?"

"It was too much, Jake." Uncle C looked up, the starlight filling his eyes. "What they'd done to her was . . . well. And it took too long to get her to the doctors. So yes, she . . . died."

"But the house?" Billy said questioningly.

"After the funeral, the man moved back in," Uncle C told him. "His friends and family said it was a bad idea, like drinking from a poisoned well. But he could still see his wife's shape in everything in that house. It must have given him strange comfort. He had the rooms cleaned out and tried to get on with his life. But sleep came with difficulty. He kept being jarred awake by an awful sound—it went *tap, tap, tap, tap, tap.*"

Uncle C tapped notes in the air with his finger.

"The sound of a knife tapping the window, signalling the other men to come in. The taps echoed throughout the house, and inside the man's head. He'd get up and go down to the kitchen window, and in the sink he would find three drops of blood. No more, no less. Still wet. He'd wipe them away but the next night—again the tapping, again the blood."

"His own wife was haunting him?"

"No, Jake," my uncle said. "His wife—or the psychic remainders of her—was trapped. Houses hold on to things. Grip fast the violence and terror, sponge them up until the wood and concrete is saturated with it. The house was her prison, you see? And so . . . so . . ."

"The man burnt it down," Lex said softly.

My uncle gave a curt nod, as if thankful to Lex for finishing the thought he'd been struggling with. "One night he couldn't bear it any longer. He lit the curtains, the mattress, lit all the boxes he'd never bothered to unpack that held the remnants of their old life together. It was the only way to release the woman he loved. The wind blows strong up here— you feel it? He watched it go up. His wife, his dream of the life they were meant to live together. Gone. When the roof caved in, he got into his car and drove away. Nobody ever saw him again."

My uncle stood and walked the beam into the torched kitchen. He outlined a square in the air with his fingers. "This was where the window used to be. Looking out over the water. The most calming, restorative view, don't you think?"

"Go on, boys," Lex said, watching my uncle. "Take a walk for a few minutes, will you?"

The long grass raked my legs as Billy and I picked our way down to the reservoir. The sky was pricked with stars. The grass gave way to a sandy shelf fringing the water. The wind was cool now, laced with the taste of autumn.

"Your uncle is a sad man, Jake."

I didn't know what to say. Uncle C had never seemed sad before that summer—if anything, he had seemed unusually delighted by the mysteries of our world.

"Everyone gets sad sometimes," I said.

"Do you get sad?" asked Billy.

Sadness was always looming in me at that age, and I expected Billy would bring it out before long, once the school year started and he abandoned me.

"I guess so. Do you get sad?" I asked.

Billy picked a dandelion and blew on it, scattering fluff. "I miss Slave Lake . . . the good parts. Miss my setsuné. But I like it here. I never had a white friend before."

"I've never had an Indian friend."

"Métis. Dene, on my mom's side."

"Oh," I said. "I'm Irish. Like, one-quarter, I think."

After a while we tromped back up the hill. As we drew nearer, Lex and my uncle came into sight. They were both sunk down on their knees. My steps faltered until Billy collided with my shoulder.

My uncle Calvin was weeping. Starlight silvered the tears on his cheeks. Lex's arms were wrapped around him, as if, should he let go, my uncle might shudder to bits.

"My fault," Lex was saying to my uncle. "I never should have allowed us to . . ."

A dark stone pressed somewhere beneath my lungs, making it hard to breathe.

Uncle C's shoulders heaved, arms jerking at nothing. Lex smoothed down his hair with one hand, then turned to see us standing there.

"Go to my van and get the blanket and pillow," he said.

I remember the blanket was extra-thick, made of horsehair. Lex draped it around my uncle's shoulders and tucked it under his legs.

"Are you okay?" I asked Uncle C.

When my uncle didn't respond, Lex said, "He'll be okay. It'll all be forgotten by the morning. He'll reset."

I remember thinking that the word "reset" was strange. It was the word my father used when a blackout swept through the neighbourhood and all the clocks in our house stopped. Lex went to the van and returned with a jug of water and a sandwich wrapped in waxed paper. He placed them next to my uncle.

"Get your bikes," he told me and Billy.

"But—"

"No buts. Your uncle's gonna be fine. I promise. I'll come right back after I drop you off at home. For now, just let him . . . Let's go."

We put our bikes in Lex's van. Its headlights washed over the house, pinning Uncle C in their glare. He stared back hollowly, his pupils so dilated that his eyes appeared jet-black.

Lex drove Billy and me into town. I felt stunned, unsure what had transpired—even though I could sense the outline of the evening's horribleness. It was like seeing things squirming under a silk sheet and knowing instinctively that if you were to pull it back you'd see thousands of centipedes crawling over each other.

Lex pulled up at Billy's house. We said our wordless goodbyes.

"Do me a favour, will you?" Lex said as he drove me home. "Don't tell your folks about tonight. It would just make them upset. Your mother especially."

What could I say to my folks anyway? "Okay, Mr. Galbraith. I won't tell."

"Good lad."

Lex patted my shoulder. I left him chewing his lip and staring through the windshield with a look on his face I couldn't read.

I know that look now, having seen it often enough in the mirror. It's the look of someone who feels helpless, unable to care for someone close to them.

6.

_____

BLACK AGNES

My tenth surgery, my third unassisted, addressed a tumour in the brain of a thirteen-year-old boy. Though benign, his tumour was enrobed by blood vessels, one of which burst during the operation when my sucker wand pushed a micron too far into its venous wall. I tried clipping the torn vessel, and I even cut the flow of blood to the patient's brain to apply a microdermal stent. When it failed to hold, I cauterized the tissues—a messy last-ditch effort—while my anesthetist injected coagulant in hopes of stopping the flow of blood from the boy's skull.

The boy was jarringly handsome, with ebony hair: Dove Yellowbird's hair, I recall thinking with dry horror. He bled to death on the table. I forced myself to stitch his scalp afterwards, a task usually given to a resident after a successful operation. I was beset by a soul-sickening serenity. I imagine it must be similar to the cold-eyed calm a drunk driver feels upon realizing that the *thump* against the side of his car was, in fact, someone's body.

I left my car in the parking lot, took a taxi home and slipped into bed beside my wife.

"How did it go?" she asked from her cocoon of sleep. She knew the operation had been nagging at me the past few days, as they all did back then.

"Fine," I lied, not wishing to disclose my massive failure to her.

Her lips found mine in the dark. "Love you, handsome."

No sooner had I closed my eyes than the screams began. They came from our two-year-old son. By then I'd learned to differentiate his screams: the scream of pain, the grouchy screech.

This one was different. It was a scream of primal fear.

My wife and I raced blindly down the hall to find him standing on his bed, arms thrashing as though he was covered in stinging ants. For an instant, my panicked impression was that he *was* covered in ants or cockroaches or earwigs that had crawled up through the vents. I flicked on the light and saw his face—his flesh a scalded red, eyes full of confused terror.

My wife gathered him into her arms and calmed him. As I had the following day off, we agreed I'd sleep with him. I carried him into the spare bedroom. "Just a bad dream, sport," I said. He was too young to articulate his nightmare, but isn't that often difficult even for adults? He tucked himself against my stomach. I draped an arm around him as his breathing settled into limp sniffles. As he drifted off, safe and warm, I thought, *I won't always be able to protect you from the things that can really hurt you, buddy.*

I knew there would be nothing I could do to protect him from cancers, cars driven by drunks, men in vans lurking down dark alleys—or, worse and more likely, the very human failures of the sort I'd fallen prey to that evening. No, I couldn't save my son from the as-yet-unknown elements of his own genome or disposition that could lead him down dangerous roads. I wouldn't always be there to steer him down the safer path—and anyway, there would come a time when he might not accept my guidance.

i.

The summer would end with my dad and me slumped together on a docking bench at the Niagara Regional Police station—my father with an eye swollen shut, me sporting a mottled bruise on my neck and a split lip.

The trouble started innocuously enough the Thursday after our last Ghost Club. Billy had showed up at my place. He was off to Woolco to buy school supplies for the upcoming year. We rode to the store together and walked its picked-over aisles. Billy bought all no-name or economy brands: a plain blue binder instead of a Trapper Keeper, Hillsbro coloured pencils instead of Crayola. He bought last year's pencil case, with a picture of Sloth from *The Goonies*—*Hey, you guuuys!*—and loaded everything into an olive canvas backpack.

On the way home, we sat on the curb so Billy could sharpen his pencils. He did so meticulously. The shavings accumulated between his legs, Billy blowing on each pencil-tip before slotting it back into the case. The process gave him immense satisfaction.

Phiff!

The sound came from behind us. I craned my head to spot a slender metal tube jutting from an upstairs window in the house at our backs.

Three facts collided in my head:

Fact 1: Percy Elkins lived in that house. How had I not recognized that?

Fact 2: Percy Elkins was the sort of boy who'd own a BB gun.

Fact 3: Percy Elkins *did* own a BB gun, and he'd just shot at us with it from his bedroom window.

Grabbing Billy, I ducked behind an oak bordering the sidewalk. I was still processing the fact that anyone, even a soul as vile as Percy Elkins, could be shooting at us in broad daylight.

"What?" Billy said when I finally spat out what was happening. "Wait, *who*?"

"Percy Elkins. He's the worst."

Billy's jaw set in the same hard line I'd seen back at the scrapyard—then he blinked, and the hardness smoothed out.

"Let's just go, Jake."

Phiff!

A BB ricocheted off the tree. Trollish laughter drifted from the window.

"Okay, but we better run super-quick."

We came out from behind the tree with our backs hunched so as to present as small a target as possible. I'd picked up my bike and was hopping on when—

Phiff!

The BB hit me in the throat. My flesh went cold before the pain receptors blinked on. My hands flew to my neck. I was sure the BB had gone right through—and soon blood would start to fountain out of my throat, turning me into a gruesome human sprinkler.

Billy pried my hands away from the wound. "No blood—wait, sorry. A little."

Staring at my blood on Billy's hands suffused me with an anger more intense than I'd ever known. Mindless and hungering, that breed of blinding rage that makes people murder one another. Taking two steps onto the grass, I grabbed a loose brick from the edge of the Elkinses' cobbled driveway and hurled it. It sailed end-over-end and hit the bay window of casa de Elkins.

The glass imploded with a weird inhalation, as if the window frame had taken a deep breath. This was followed by a musical tinkling as broken shards fell onto the floorboards. The wind picked up, blowing the curtains back into the Elkinses' living room, catching on points of glass glittering in the frame.

"Holy shit," said Billy.

The front door opened. Percy stood in the doorway with his pellet gun. Terry Vreeland loomed behind him.

"You're going to pay for that," said Percy.

At first, I thought he was threatening to beat me up. Then the truth dawned: he wanted me to pay for a new window.

"I'm not," I surprised myself by saying. "You shot me."

A sneer from Percy. "Where's your proof?"

I tilted my neck towards him, showing off the bloody redness.

"Could've been a bee, you big fat shit."

Billy steadied my head in his hands. When I flinched, he told me, "It's okay, steady."

Gingerly, he dug the BB out of my neck and squeezed it between his thumb and forefinger. He turned to Percy, displaying it. Percy put the gun down and stepped from his house.

"Gimme it."

He held his hand out for the BB.

"Why would I?" said Billy.

"It's my property."

Even as kids, we understood that once an object had been lodged in someone else's skin, its ownership transferred to the afflicted party. Billy put the bloody pellet in his pocket.

"Give that here, stupid," Percy said. When Billy refused, Percy appealed to me. "Tell him to give it over, fat ass."

"Don't give it to him, Billy." My voice was remarkably calm but I felt as though my skin was about to burst into flames.

"Go get it, Terr," Percy said.

Terry took a tentative step towards Billy . . . but something in Billy's demeanour, the way his head was cocked as if to say, *Come on if you're coming*, stopped the bigger boy.

"Dunno, Perse," Terry said. "You did kinda put it in Jake's neck."

"You were on my property," Percy sniffed at me, turning lawyerly. "I was protecting my . . . my land."

What was he, a farmer? I said, "You can't shoot us for that."

"Can too. I can do anything I want on my property."

As absurd as such an argument would sound to an adult, as kids, faced with Percy's slick legalese, we were almost hoodwinked.

"The oak tree isn't your property," I said, uncertain now.

Percy walked to the edge of the curb and raked his heel across the dirt, the way you did in the schoolyard to etch the base paths for stickball. "Everything inside this is my property. I can do whatever I want."

Billy said, "We were just sitting here sharpening pencils."

Percy shrugged as if that made no difference. "You looked suspicious. I was protecting my belongings. Now you have to pay for my window."

He drew himself up to his full, if underwhelming, height. He even hooked his thumbs under his armpits, as I'm sure he'd seen crafty lawyers do in TV shows.

"If you don't fix my window, I'll call the cops and they'll take you away to juvie."

I hated how Percy appended *my* to everything: *my* property, *my* window. Meanwhile, I stood with *my* blood dripping down *my* neck while Percy preened, now standing with his arms smugly crossed.

"You're lying," I said, emboldened by another jolt of rage. "You shot me in the neck. You're lucky it wasn't my eye. I busted your window. Even Steven. Let's go, Billy."

Percy's face soured. He stepped off the curb and slugged me in the face.

His fist made a flat *smack* on my nose. I staggered back on my heels but didn't fall down. I straightened, blinking the water out of my eyes, and saw Billy getting ready to jump in. He could have flattened both Terry and Percy, though I didn't know it back then. But this wasn't Billy's fight. All the fear and rage— the lingering sting of the BB, every casual torment I'd suffered at Percy's hands—came together in my arms and shoulders, a thousand strings tightening towards a point of intent.

Percy stood there with his hands down, unaware. I put my not-insubstantial weight on my forward leg, torqued my hips and slung my fist around—

I hit him in the nose. And it exploded. That's the only word for it. Percy's nose had a sharp point, so when my fist struck the bridge, the cartilage . . . blew up.

Yes, Percy's nose shattered like his window had, but with a buckling sound like the dent popping out of a garbage can lid. He toppled back on his lawn, hands flying up to his face. When he saw the blood on them, he shrieked like a seagull and fled inside.

I'd never hit anyone before, let alone a budding sociopath like Percy. It felt good, *really* good. Billy and I hightailed it out of there. Billy's house was closer but I was worried about the blowback, so we agreed to split up.

"You sure you're okay, Jake?" he asked.

"I'm okay."

Billy gave me the BB. He was still a bit stunned. "I can't believe you . . . holy *shit*."

Once I got back to my house I phoned my father at work.

"Calm down, sport, tell me what happened."

When I told him that I'd been in a fight, he chuckled disbelievingly. Then I told him about the pellet gun.

"That boy shot you?" My father's voice held a quivering edge.

"Only with a BB, but—"

"Sit tight. I'll be right home."

Ten minutes later, my father's car slewed into the

driveway. He got out and rolled up his shirt sleeves. He tilted my chin in his hands to inspect the mark on my neck: a purpling bruise with a nugget of crusted blood in the centre. I handed my father the BB. Dad held it in his palm, the metal ball still red with my blood.

"Where does this boy live?" he asked in a stilted monotone. "I ought to have a—a little chat with his father."

As it turned out, my father wouldn't have to make the trip. The creech of tires came to us over the maples and soon a land-whale of a car was tear-assing down our road. The driver hammered on the brakes, leaving strips of smoking rubber on the street.

"Hey!" a man said, getting out. "Hey, you, goddamn it!"

Percy Elkins's father looked nothing like his son: he was hulking where Percy was scrawny, flushed where Percy was milk-pale. He wore a button-up shirt like my father's, except the sleeves were short. On his feet were workboots instead of penny loafers. I remember Percy boasting that his dad was a construction foreman, which I figured meant he sat in a trailer on construction sites eyeballing blueprints and long rows of numbers.

"You the one?" he said, pointing a hairy-knuckled finger at me. "You the little bastard who busted my window and my boy's nose?"

He advanced like a runaway locomotive. What I was aware of even more, however, was my father's reaction—which was no visible reaction at all. His arms hung loosely at his sides and his expression remained the same except for a vague contraction at the corners of his eyes. He looked bored, actually, like a man waiting for a bus to arrive.

Mercifully, it was over fast. Mr. Elkins swung at my father with a fist roughly the size of a summer squash. My dad didn't bother to dodge. He *let* a 250-pound man hit him in the face. He rocked back, his knees unhinging, and touched the driveway with his ass— then just as fast as he'd fallen he was back up, resurrected, pinioning off the tarmac with one arm, already working the violent impulse into his body, his knees flexing, spine whipsawing to generate momentum.

My father brought his fist down in a chopping motion like a man slamming a trap door. His knuckles hit flush on Mr. Elkins's chin. The big man fell forward and just kept falling, as if his soul had suddenly been sucked out of him. He hit the driveway face first.

Dad said, "Get some ice, Jake. He's going to wake up with a headache."

By the time the cops showed up, Mr. Elkins was slumped behind the wheel of his car with a broken nose. He made a matching pair with Percy, who sat in the passenger seat. Percy's father had accepted the bag of ice from my father with whipped-dog gratitude. I had the bruise on my neck and Dad's eye was puffed up—but overall, you had to chalk it up as a win for the Baker clan.

Sitting on that bench in the police station later that afternoon, Dad threw an arm around my shoulders. "I'm glad you hit back," he said, one eye puffed so completely shut that it looked like he was tipping me a gruesome wink. "Tell you this—you'll suffer less in life if you swing back. Only if you're pushed to it, of course. And I'd say someone pegging you with a BB is a mighty big push. Give as much as you get. Doesn't matter if you fall. All that matters is, you get up again."

The legal matter was resolved quickly. No charges were laid, and Mr. Elkins was on the hook for his own window. My mother showed up as we were signing the witness papers, all set to give us hell—until Mrs. Elkins came through the door. A woman of imposing carriage, she carried a purse as big as a grocery sack. Seeing her beside Mr. Elkins, I wondered how Percy could have ended up as such a sparrow-chested, noodle-armed bonerack.

"Our son's nose is broken," Mrs. Elkins said to her husband, as if this might come as news to him. "The doctor says he'll have a bump the rest of his life."

She wheeled on my family, purse swinging on her arm. Something rattled inside it and I imagined Tic Tacs: boxes and boxes of Tic Tacs, the nasty orange ones.

"Our son's nose is now ruined," she said to my mother, "at your son's hands. And then your husband attacks my husband like some kind of crazed animal."

Mr. Elkins, his own nose in a splint, laid a hand on his wife's shoulder. "Dora—"

Mrs. Elkins shrugged her husband's hand away and rose menacingly over my mother.

"Well? What about my son's nose?"

Mom, who'd come into the situation cold, glanced at me with my bruised neck and my father with his purpled eye. She calmly addressed Mrs. Elkins.

"Honestly, my dear, I find myself struggling to care."

Even the cops had a laugh at that.

ii.

That night, pebbles struck my bedroom window. A pinworm of dread threaded into my heart. Maybe it was Percy down in the yard, and the pebbles would be followed by bricks.

I sat up in bed and cracked the window open. Dove stood in the shadow of our backyard hemlock.

"Hey."

"Hay is for horses," she whispered. "The moon's up and so am I. Come with me, child. Fulfill your destiny and become a creature of *zee night*."

"Come with you and do what?"

She shrugged, leaving it up to me. Moonlight fell through the hemlock and shone off the mirror of her hair . . . and I found myself very much awake.

I pulled on my clothes, crept down to the garage and pushed my bike out. Dove put her hand on the side of my face, rolling my chin to inspect the bruise Percy's BB had left.

"Yow," she said. "Billy said it was bad. Look on the bright side—not many guys can get shot in the neck and then knock out the guy who shot them."

"I didn't knock him out."

"Give you a tip, Jake." Her fingers hadn't left my neck. My pulse quickened under her touch. "Anyone else asks, tell them you knocked the little bastard out. Because if nobody can prove it didn't happen, hell, it may as well be true. Never wake the dreamers from their dream."

We rode through the suburbs, the ticking of our gears the only sound. I'd rarely been out this late, and never without my parents. Everything lay in a wrap of shadows. I felt an ownership of the night, and perhaps a whole world that didn't exist in daytime.

We cut down a path tapering through the woods. The forest was alive with movement—I glimpsed the furred rump of a raccoon bumbling into a thicket—which would have petrified me under normal circumstances, but now, with Dove, and after the day I'd had, that fear was absent. The path spat us onto the public golf course. We biked over the eighth fairway, skirting the sand trap, following an alloyed moon. We had to hop off our bikes and squeeze through a gap in the railing near the Pro Shop, riding up a gravel drive that led to Stanley Avenue.

The oaks of the Niagara public links rose like broken fingers against the street-lit sky. The expensive hotels rose in columns of cold light to the south, and beyond them the falls were lit by green spotlights, the water rushing endlessly, siphoning away those precious tourist dollars.

The local marine theme park, Land of Oceans, lay across the road. The parking lot was empty save for a lone camper van with Texas plates. We rode along the fence till we reached the staff entrance and hopped the locked gate, following a path behind the deer park.

"Let's check out the whales," Dove said.

We cut through the picnic area and over the train tracks, our reflections travelling the panes of glass of the Happy Manatee restaurant. The water of the killer whale pool lay black behind the two-inch-thick spectators' glass. The sickle of a whale's dorsal fin slit the water. Then the whale glided past, the white patch surrounding its eye glowing like a lantern in a cave.

Dove threw open the gate that led to a footbridge spanning the pool.

"I'm going, that's it, I'm doing it."

Her voice ascended on the second-to-last word, elongating it—I'm *dooooo-ing* it—as she skipped lightly across the bridge. Before my mind could catalogue the risks, which included but were not limited to tripping and falling into a pool containing two enormous unpredictable mammals, I was following her.

Imagine trying to hold the tail of a comet as it blazes across the heavens. It's burning your hands, eating you up, but there's no malice in it; a comet can't possibly know or care about you. You will sacrifice all you are or ever will be for that comet because it suffuses every inch of your skin with a sweet itch you cannot scratch, and through its grace you discover velocities you never dreamt possible. You will love that comet, but part of that love—a percentage impossible to calibrate—is tied to your inability to understand it. How can that comet burn as it does, pursue the trajectory it does? It confuses you, because the comet disguises itself as a human girl. But make no mistake, the girl contains fire to evaporate oceans, light to blind minor gods. If I could freeze her in the heartbeat where she skipped across the footbridge, carve her out of time and fix her in the firmament . . . in the deepest chambers of my heart, I know that nobody, not another soul on earth, will ever be as purely astonishing as Dove Yellowbird was in that moment.

My reflection quivered in the water under the bridge and then, miraculously, I was over. Dove danced across the show stage. A whale bobbed up at the pool's edge, its head sleek as a ballistic torpedo.

Dove said, "Every year in Slave Lake they string nets across the river during the salmon run. I'd sit on the banks watching them leap. Almost all of them jumped into the net, but every so often one made it over. I felt happy for it, until I stopped to think. All that salmon's family and friends were back in the net, right?" She gestured at the whales. "These guys are the ones who got caught in the net. Their families are out at sea."

The whale's mouth yawned open to reveal teeth blunted with age and disuse. Dove reached down—

"Dove!"

Her fingertips grazed the whale's chin, its skin scuffed from rubbing against the sides of the pool. The whale flicked its head and dipped below the water.

"We should set them free." Dove laughed, presumably at how silly the idea was: freeing a pair of whales trapped in a tank two thousand miles from the nearest ocean. "Is that crazy?"

"Maybe so."

She grabbed my hand. Contrails of comet-heat smoked in her eyes.

"Crazy or not, you'd help me, wouldn't you?"

Of course, Dove. Anything you ever ask.

We crossed back over the bridge, heading towards our bikes. There were rumours that the owner of Land of Oceans often circuited the park at night in his truck. He had a shotgun and would shoot whatever he found on his premises. Raccoons, possums . . . kids?

"I like you, Jake," Dove said abruptly. "You don't put on any kind of act. You're not cool and you don't think you are."

"Thanks."

"I don't mean it like that, dummy. I'm just saying that you're real, y'know? And believe me, you'll get tired of me before I get tired of you."

"I don't think so," I mumbled, making it sound more a question. *I don't think so?*

She laughed. "If you could, like, slap a tag on me and put me on a shelf—you know what that tag would say?"

"What?"

"'Somewhat damaged.'"

Even back then, in my confusion over this strange new bend in our conversation, I'd thought, *Who of us isn't damaged?*

"And if you don't get tired of me, Jake, your folks will put an end to it."

"Why would they?" I said.

"Haven't you figured it out yet? I'm the girl your mother warned you about."

Neither of us heard the growl of the engine until the truck swung round almost directly behind us. Its lights snapped on, pinning us like moths on a sheet.

"Run, Jake!"

We sprinted into the rides area. The Viking Ship rose two hundred feet away. Behind it lay scrubland thick with trees. Dove ran hard, flinging her head back, her mouth open to the sky. Despite the panic her eyes were bright and she was smiling.

I was scared—with that crystalline, childish fear of being caught and punished. That fear thrashed behind my rib cage like a bird in cupped hands, perhaps the last truly childlike instance of that emotion I'd ever feel. That fear is a kind of magic. As you get older, the texture of your fear changes. You're no longer afraid of the things you had absolute faith in as a child: that you'd die in convulsions from inhaling the gas from a shattered light bulb, that chewing apple pips brought on death by cyanide poisoning, or that a circus dwarf had actually bounced off a trampoline into the mouth of a hungry hippo. You stop believing in the things my uncle believed in. Even if your mind wants to go there, it has lost the nimbleness needed to make the leap. That magic gets kicked out of you, churched out, shamed out—or worse, you steal it from yourself. It gets embarrassed out of you by the kids who run the same stretch of streets and grown-ups who say it's time to put away childish things. By degrees, you kill your own magic. Before long your fears become adult ones: crushing debts and responsibilities, sick parents and sick kids, the possibility of dying unremembered or unloved. Fears of not being the person you were so certain you'd grow up to be.

Looking back, I wish I'd relished those final instants of childish fear: that saccharine-sweet taste of terror curdling like sour milk in my mouth.

We'd nearly reached the Viking Ship. We redlined for the final kick. Dove arched her spine and craned her neck in the posture of a marathoner snapping the tape at the finish line. The safety of the trees loomed. I imagined I heard a shotgun breech being snapped open over the roar of the truck's engine—

We raced into the bushes. The truck's headlights washed the foliage as we backed deeper into the cover of the trees. The door opened. Boots *pink-pinked* on the cobbles. A shape stepped in front of the headlights as a flashlight swept left to right. Dove yanked me down. The earth had a mulchy-sweet smell. The flashlight flicked off. The owner retreated to his truck and drove off.

"The winners." Dove raised her arms like a triumphant boxer, making the noise of an appreciative crowd. "*Raaaah, raaaaaaah.*"

We walked to a clearing where the grass stood washed in moonlight. We collapsed on the ground and lay side by side, still breathing hard.

"How do you want to be posed in your coffin?"

"What?"

Dove rolled over to face me. A maple key was stuck to her cheek. I wanted to pluck that key off but couldn't quite find the courage.

"Like, yeah, when you die," she said. "Most people go for this one." She demonstrated, lying flat on her back with her hands crossed over her chest in a classic Nosferatu pose. "But I want something rock 'n' roll, like this." Arms still crossed, she flipped the bird with both hands, mouth set in a Billy Idol sneer. "Like that, right? Screw you, Reaper, I'm still cool as balls."

I laughed and said, "You'd have a rocking funeral."

"What about you? Show me."

I experimented with a few poses before settling on one where my hands were clawed in front of my face, which was set in a rictus of stunned terror.

"What the hell happened to you?"

"Got buried alive."

"Oooh, primo. Someone's getting fired, big time." Dove shrugged. "Somebody told me that morticians wouldn't be allowed to twist our faces and pose us that way."

I could smell her breath: Dentyne cinnamon gum and something else, something electric. I thought she was going to kiss me. I'd never been kissed except by my parents and old aunties. I thought, *Maybe this is how it happens*. It felt like it ought to happen, if only because I wanted it so badly.

"I've got to get out of this city, Jake. Hook up with some guy with a motorcycle and long hair. I'm flexible on hair length but the motorcycle is a must. No offence, but this place bores me to tears."

I blinked. My whole body blinked. Was this girl— who'd recently stuck her hand in a killer whale's mouth—telling me she was bored? Worse was the fact that she wanted to blow town in the company of a ponytailed biker. She must've read my thoughts when she opened her eyes and saw my face. Her own features projected shock, which softened into concern.

"Oh, Jake."

Oh, Jake. Guilty, regretful. *Jake, you glad-hearted fool.*

"Oh, no, it's just . . ." She smiled pacifyingly. "The things I want from life are different from the things you want."

"I want the same things you do," I protested.

But something so ineffably hurt and broken crossed her face that I didn't say anything more. Taking my hand, she said, "This much is true: I could pass into the long dark with you."

"The long dark?"

"That's what my setsuné called it. Death. She never talked about it that way to Billy, Billy's too sensitive, but that's how she saw it. Blackness smooth as oil, stretching into forever. She said you got to think hard about whose hand you're holding when that darkness takes hold. Someone strong, solid, with a good heart."

"So, you want me to hold your hand when you die?"

Squeezing my hand tighter, she said, "Will you hold me as I die, Jake . . . wait, what's your middle name?"

"Clarence."

"Clarence?"

"My uncle's middle name."

"Calvin Clarence?"

"Uh-huh."

When she spoke next, it was in mimicry of a minister at a wedding. "Do you, Jake Clarence Baker, swear to hold Dove Petunia Yellowbird's hand as she sheds this mortal coil?"

"Petunia?"

"I'm screwing around. I don't have a middle name. Do you promise, though? Promise you'll usher me into the long dark?"

"I do."

"Then by the power vested in me, I knight thee, dub thee, whatever-the-hell thee, both death partners until the day you shall, uhh, yeah, die."

There are still days when I'll drift back to the instant when, disoriented by Percy Elkins's exploding firework, I'd seen Dove standing in the schoolyard with a skateboard slung like an axe over her shoulder. Years later, I assisted on an operation where a surgeon many times my superior unblocked a neural pathway to give a four-year-old girl sight. I was there when she opened her eyes. The moment she saw her parents and brother—who before then had been merely voices—she broke into an astounded cascade of giggles. That was the closest I can come to my own sense of seeing Dove that first time: something unlocked inside me and these fresh possibilities flooded in, opening my whole world up.

I'd never fall for anyone as hard as I fell for Dove Yellowbird. You always fall hardest the first time, don't you? There's no bottom to it. As I reached teenagehood and beyond, I'd hear guys say: *I just don't get women*. And sure, I didn't get women either, but wasn't that the best part, the not knowing? Where else could that wild, passionate, scream-it-from-the-rooftops love come from?

iii.

Another school year rolled around. At first, I thought this meant the taunting and bullying would start up again. Another year of hanging out by the monkey bars trying to cast a spell of invisibility on myself. But a series of minor seismic events would lead to a different social situation that year, and I soon found that I no longer dreaded the school bell.

For one, Percy left me alone. The first day of school he showed up with a splint on his nose. It turned out his doctor was right: there would always be a bump on it, the bump I'd put there. I hoped he'd think of me every time he glanced in the mirror.

Second, there was Billy. He was in my grade, same class. I kept waiting for him to find better friends, but that never happened. Then as now, Billy was Billy; if he liked you, he stuck by you. It didn't matter to Billy that I was a pariah. He retained that stillness I had seen in the summer, but at school it translated as cool. Billy Yellowbird was *mysterious*, man, and that shine rubbed off on me.

That fall, for the first time, I wasn't picked dead last for kickball. I was picked second-to-last, a colossal step up. I discovered that I could ask to borrow a slice of paper from a classmate and, wonder of wonders, actually get one . . . still, I brought my own paper just in case.

I didn't go mad with this new-found status. I hung out with Billy, paying him back in whatever small ways I could. We'd sit in my garage after school reading *Creep Show* comics and copies of *Fortean Times*. I helped him prepare for math tests. He applied himself with the same intensity with which he approached all endeavours and gradually he got better. Ours was a small, contained universe and I was happy within it.

It was late September and I was biking home after visiting Billy one Saturday afternoon, tires crunching through drifts of early autumn leaves, when I spotted Uncle C on a bus bench at the corner of Dunn and Hagar.

I hadn't seen him since the night at the burnt house. Looking back, I can see that my avoidance had been purposeful. Sure, I could say I was preoccupied with Billy and Dove—and that wasn't exactly untrue—but the deeper truth was that the Ghost Club meetings, especially the final few, had left me unsettled. Still, I'd stopped by the Occultorium once or twice since that night on the hill. It was always locked. One time I saw the red light flashing on the Bat Phone as it rang inside the empty shop. I hoped that Dark Heshie and the Watcher and the rest of Uncle C's network weren't having separation anxiety. He hadn't come by the house for our regular Sunday dinners in a while. When I asked my mother about this, she said, "Your uncle comes and goes as he pleases," and would say no more.

My uncle gestured me over. "We've got one final mission, Jake. Tonight."

I hesitated. The Ghost Club had been a summer thing, hadn't it? But there was something about Uncle C—maybe it was the anxious twitch of his fingers, as if he was plucking the strings of a guitar— that forced me to consider his proposal. "Where are we going?"

We made plans to meet at the graveyard at seven, just the two of us. He promised I'd be home in time for bed. That evening as I sat pushing my mashed potatoes around the plate, Mom put down her fork and said, "Why so glum, chum?"

I'm not sure why I chose that moment to tell my folks, after keeping the club a secret all summer—but I did. Told them everything. Head down, eyes on the tabletop. When I got to the part about leaving Uncle

C at the burnt house, my mother pushed away from the table and left the kitchen.

"This was such a *baaaad* idea, Jake," my father said. "And that you'd keep it all to yourself—goddamn, that's not like you at all."

When Mom returned, the skin around her eyes was red and puffy, and she had a plan. "What you're going to do, Jake," she said with uncanny calm, "is go to the cemetery tonight. Your father and I will come, too—not with you, but behind you."

"Why? Is something the matter with Uncle C?"

"We'll tell you the whole story," my mother said. "We should've told you a while ago, but it's complicated, and right now we don't have time."

I set off to meet Uncle C at a quarter to seven. Mom and Dad were going to follow in the car. I felt treacherous, like a snitch wearing a wire.

My uncle waited at the Fairview Cemetery gates. His face was furred with a Brillo-pad beard—which was strange, because he had always been clean-shaven, ever since I could remember—and he exuded a new smell, musty and a little stale. I know now that it's the smell of age, nothing else, just the un-maskable smell every human body develops over time.

We stepped through the gates, breezing past rows of gravestones so old that the wind and rain had scrubbed the names and dates away.

Uncle C said, "How's school going?"

I told him that things were pretty okay, actually.

"That's good, Jake. You're a good kid, and you'll be a fine man. People will be drawn to you, just you watch."

We continued through the graveyard to reach a statue of a hooded woman with her arms outstretched. Her stone eyes gazed at the sky. Green mould crawled the folds of her robe where it spread across the grave plinth.

"Her name is Black Agnes, Jake. Ever hear of her?"

When I shook my head, my uncle said, "She used to live around here way back in horse and buggy days. With her husband and young daughter in a homestead along the river. They had a good life, but it was a dangerous time. You had disease and starvation and calamity or . . . or drowning, say."

He cleared his throat of some hidden obstruction and went on. "Black Agnes's daughter was down by the river one day, running far ahead of her mother. Then as now, the banks were treacherous. The rocks may as well be covered in grease. It happened too fast for her mother to even know she was gone, Jake. After a while, Agnes followed the path down to the river, calling her daughter's name, and saw a white ribbon stuck on a thorn bush near the water. The same one her daughter wore in her hair. Just that lonely ribbon and the deep, endless river."

The Long Dark. Dove's words formed on a movie theatre screen in my mind, hovering there weightlessly.

"To lose a child, Jake . . . nothing worse. Especially
like that. To lose sight of her for what must've seemed
like a *second*. Gone. Disappeared. Drowned probably. Ninety-nine-point-nine percent sure, right? But
there'd always be that niggling worry. What if the
river spat her up five miles down? Had she staggered
from the water, coughing and retching, to find . . .
who knows what could have happened? Sometimes,
Jake, disappeared is worse than dead. With dead, at
least there's an end.

"After that, Agnes wasn't the same. She never had
another child to replace the one she'd lost. She grew
silent and introspective. She'd wander the riverbanks
calling her daughter's name. She'd go at night, barefoot
in the chill, coming home shivering with mud caked
on her nightgown. That's how she got her name, Black
Agnes—because she was always out in the blackness
looking for something never to be found. Five years
after her daughter's disappearance, Agnes died. Her
husband buried her here and had this statue built."

My uncle reached up as if to touch the statue's
outstretched hand . . . but his hand recoiled before
making contact with the stone.

"The legend of Black Agnes is a different matter
altogether. It came from a dare, long after Agnes had

been buried. One of those silly dares teenagers egg each other into. A local girl's friends goaded her into spending a night in this graveyard, sitting right here, beside the statue. She was terrified, but peer pressure's a terrible thing. The next morning the girl was discovered in the statue's arms. An autopsy revealed that she'd been squeezed to death. Her internal organs were pulped, her bones shattered. As if she'd been hugged."

Uncle C's eyes found mine through the granular light. I couldn't tell if he believed this story. He may have, but I didn't. And that was the first time I felt it. A subtle pulling apart.

"She'd been wrapped up in arms of stone, so the legend goes. The arms of Black Agnes, who'd mistaken the girl for her long-lost daughter and hugged her so protectively that she'd crushed the life right out of her."

A flashlight's beam swept the tombstones off to the east. I heard Mom's voice.

"Jake? Cal? You over here?"

Uncle C gave me a shocked and injured glance. I can see that expression still. I figure I'll carry it with me the rest of my life. *So you sold me down the river, eh, Jakey-boy?*

My mother and father stepped into view. "Oh," my uncle said, "it's both of you."

"Just enjoying the night air, Cal," Dad said with a strained laugh.

We stood in front of Black Agnes. My mother took her brother's hand. "You okay?"

My uncle smiled. "Never better, sis."

She spoke tenderly. "Black Agnes, huh?"

Uncle C seemed surprised. "You know about her?"

"You told me all about her, Calvin."

"I did? Can't say I remember that."

"Maybe it wasn't you," my mother said.

She took the flashlight my father had brought along and aimed the beam ten feet away from the statue of Black Agnes.

LYDIA SHARPE

1949–1975

Mom pinned the flashlight beam on the tombstone. My uncle stared at it. Many different things seemed to pass over his face.

"She's got our last name," he said after a long gulf of silence. "You know her?"

"I might have," Mom said. "Lots of Sharpes in this city. What about you?"

My uncle's upper lip twitched. It was almost a snarl, as if some predatory animal had momentarily seized control of his features.

"Doesn't ring a bell," he said in a detached voice. "Like you said, lot of Sharpes around. Lydia. Nice name." He laughed distractedly. "You know what, sis? Maybe I *did* know a . . . nope. Not coming to me."

My mother said: "No use racking our brains over it, Cal. Listen, we've got to get Jake home. School night."

"Okay, sis," Uncle C said, his voice dreamy now. "I got my bike."

"Sam, why don't you take Jake home? I'll walk with Cal."

We left the cemetery as a foursome. Thunder bristled over the falls. When we reached the sidewalk Mom and Uncle C went one way, while my father and I went the other.

"And so it ends, huh?" my uncle said to me as we parted company. "The good ole club."

"It was great," I said sincerely. "I'll never forget it."

Uncle C nodded. "It *was* great, wasn't it—because it was ours."

Dad and I walked home without speaking. Something monumental had just happened—the knowledge of this itched inside my chest, present but not yet understood.

My mother got home an hour later.

"How's Cal?" Dad asked.

"He's okay. He's . . . no, oh, I don't know."

Dad filled three mugs with cocoa powder and put the kettle on. When it shrieked he filled the mugs and stirred until the powder dissolved.

Mom said, "Would you mind Irishing mine up?"

Dad opened the cupboard over the fridge and splashed Jameson's into Mom's mug, and the same for his own. Mom took her mug and sipped, peering at me over the rim.

"Some things you leave buried hoping they stay buried, Jake," she began.

And then, for the next hour, she disinterred the story of my uncle's buried life.

iv.

Calvin Sharpe first spied Lydia Nix in the fall of 1968, when they were both freshmen at Niagara College. Lydia owned Calvin from that very first look.

If my uncle could've seen the person he'd become: the Occultorium, the tie-dyed shirts, the Bat Phone, goblins and spooks . . . if he were able to view himself apart from the circumstances that had compelled the change, well, he would have found it perplexing. According to my mother, Calvin was, at that time, an "evidence of his eyes" sort of fellow.

If it could be seen and touched and tabulated, then it was real.

He attended college to study physics, which suited the man he was back then. Lydia would flip-flop on her major, eventually pursuing English with a minor in History. A more unlikely pair you would not find. Yin and yang, oil and water—but when it works, it works.

Lydia was beautiful, if atypically so. Her nose had been broken by a field hockey stick in high school, which gave it a bump much like the one on Percy Elkins's nose. If anything, this imperfection served to heighten the surrounding beauty. Calvin was smitten, and was shocked when Lydia returned that ardour, the way it usually shocks a middling-handsome man when an out-of-his-league woman expresses interest.

It didn't take long after they met for their differences to become evident. Lydia took Calvin to palmists and tarot card readers. He had his life-line and love-line read, and the forecast was pleasant. The Hanged Man did not loom in their future.

They fell in love. It happened naturally and easily. Calvin loved Lydia in a needful and elemental way, the way a flower loves the sun.

They graduated and moved into an apartment in Niagara Falls. Calvin went to work for a petrochemical company while Lydia worked as an in-class teacher's aide. On weekends, they went on double dates with my mother and the dangerous new man in her life, Sam Baker. Sam could be an unmerciful tease but Calvin was tolerant of it. They became a tight-knit foursome.

Calvin and Lydia married on a July afternoon in 1972. It's unlikely that Calvin ever knew a happier day in his life. They moved into a house on a hill outside the city limits—Lydia's idea, a private idyll away from it all. The pragmatist in Calvin rose up— it was too isolated, cut off from the main arteries— but then he told himself he was being a wet noodle.

Lydia became pregnant. It wasn't anything they'd been working for, just nature taking its course. Life was coming together for them, as it sometimes does for good people who make a point of being decent.

One night in late November there came a knock at the door.

The region had been rocked by a cold snap. A thick carpet of snow had fallen, and the river lay frozen twenty yards out. Lydia opened the door to find two men. Strangers. One of them told Lydia that it was rather cold outside. Could they come in? I imagine him saying this politely, even bashfully, looking at Lydia Sharpe out of the tops of his eyes.

When Lydia hesitated, the man reached into his pea coat and pulled out a long, sharp fillet knife. It would later be admitted as court's evidence in a zip-lock Baggie marked 2-A.

The papers would identify the men as Adrian Bellweather and Patrick Lucas, recent parolees from the penitentiary. Their prior misdeeds didn't paint them as the monsters they'd prove to be that night, but their young faces were hived with old, cold cunning.

What happened is impossible to say with any exactness. The known evidence is this: nothing was stolen, nothing was burnt and almost nothing was broken. The men left as they'd come, melting into the same darkness that had borne them to the front door. At the trial, when the prosecutor asked why they'd done it, the replies of both men would be couched in apathy. They saw lights burning in a house set well back from the main road. The opportunity had presented itself, that was all. It was all a game that went a smidge too far.

You could say such individuals aren't properly human. They merely drape themselves in the costume of humanity, clad in the same skin that covers everyone else's bones while inside there's nothing but wolfish hunger. After they left, Calvin waited as long as he could bear, out of a fear they might return. But Lydia was bleeding, and was well into her second trimester. Calvin carried her outside. The men had cut some wires under Calvin's car hood but he knew a bit about cars. He tried to fix it while Lydia sat in the car, getting colder. He must have been petrified the men would come back. They might have been at the forest-line, waiting until Calvin had nearly got the car started before returning to finish things.

Calvin connected the wires and tore down an unplowed road that led to town, to the hospital. The road crossed several bridges spanning the network of oxbow lakes. On the largest of these bridges, the wheel must've started to shimmy in Calvin's hands. *No no no no please no* he must have thought, but as his physics classes had taught him, an object in motion tended to stay in motion.

The car fishtailed, slammed into a barrier, pinballed back into the other, hopped the retaining wall and crashed through the ice.

It is not known what happened beneath the ice, in the frigid black. Surely Calvin tried desperately to save his wife. Surely, he'd have sacrificed himself so that Lydia and their unborn child might survive. But in the end, it was they who would remain down under the water while Calvin, through luck or providence, surfaced through the hole cleaved in the ice.

It so happened that a tow truck came along shortly thereafter. The driver saw the sheared rail, the gaping hole, the man lying unconscious beside it. Calvin was airlifted to the hospital. His cranial injuries were so severe that the surgeon put him into a medically induced coma. When Calvin woke weeks later, his hair had gone from brown to bone-white.

The first thing he said was, "Jeez, I'm hungry. I'd kill for some scrambled eggs."

He did not remember a thing. None of it. His wife. Their unborn child. Nothing.

It was difficult to pinpoint where Calvin's memories ended, or identify the cause of that loss. Physically he'd sustained massive trauma. His scalp was gashed, leaving a scar above his hairline. His skull had cracked, a hairline fissure bisecting several plates of bone. He had been under the water a long time, so there was a strong possibility that he'd suffered significant brain damage from oxygen deprivation.

The manner of his memory deficit was striking. My mother said that Calvin awoke not remembering Lydia. He could remember going to college and other events during the time when his life intersected with his wife's, but nothing of her. He retained no memory of their marriage, or of owning that house on the hill. He didn't remember the men who'd come during the storm or the car crashing through the ice. It was as if Calvin's mind clipped those memories clean off the chain of his life. His brain had created an almost seamless overlay, draped over his past: a patchwork of incidents and places and moments, some of which bore a similarity to his actual lived experience whereas others were fabricated, fantasies his mind had created to account for the times in his life when Lydia had been present. This overlay was unquestionably embraced as truth by the only person who mattered: Calvin himself.

So profound was his memory loss—was *loss* the right word? . . . memory *re-engineering* is more apt—that a clinical psychiatrist adjudged him unfit to testify at the trial of Bellweather and Lucas. The diagnosis held that it would be useless to make Calvin testify in light of the fact that he did not, and would not, admit to ever living in the house, being married to the deceased or to being terrorized by the defendants. This did not prevent the trial from going forward, where the judge handed down sentences that would see both men behind bars until they were old and frail.

You might think my chosen career would lend me insight on my uncle's condition. But while I can tell you about the brain as a physical object, such as how much it weighs (roughly three pounds), how many neurons it contains (25 billion), how large and thick it would be if it were unfolded (the size of a foam placemat), beyond that I am a glorified techie. I know the nuts and bolts and can diagnose flaws within the mainframe. While I can identify and sometimes fix structural maladies within that organ, I do not remotely understand it. That is an impossible task, like trying to guess the path rainwater will take down a windowpane. There is simply no way to know with any accuracy what is happening inside someone else's head. I only faintly comprehend what is going on inside my own.

It was my mother who made the decision. It did not come easily to her, but she decided to let Calvin live his lie. Who was it harming? My uncle's mind had settled on this act of erasure as a coping mechanism. In the short term at least, why not allow him some peace?

My uncle did not attend his wife's funeral. Why would he go to a stranger's burial? My mother and father arranged the service. Mom sold the house on the hill and had the money transferred into Calvin's account. He accepted this phantom windfall blithely.

After the incident, my uncle's personality changed. Where before he was pragmatic and literal-minded, he became a wide-eyed believer. A mystic. Fascinated with the occult, phantasmic emanations, and what "they" weren't telling us. He ditched his workman-like wardrobe for tie-dyed shirts and Cthulhu-bead bracelets. He quit his job—though he did not "quit" per se; he didn't recall working at the petrochemical company, so he just stopped showing up. He used the money from the house to buy the Occultorium, installed the Bat Phone and began taking down notes in spiral notebooks.

This kind of personality shift can happen, under certain circumstances. I've witnessed it myself in some of my patients. And none of Cal's changes were truly *bad*. As my father said, it was like the physicist Calvin had been swapped out for a bizarro-world Calvin—but he was still the same sweet, honest, loving person he'd always been.

Everyone important bought into my mother's plan. My father, if reluctantly. Lexington Galbraith, with the resigned devotion of a best friend. Their efforts became a clandestine community initiative: Operation Keep Cal in the Dark. To them, I guess it felt like mercy. Though perhaps it simply felt like love.

And it worked, for a while at least. Calvin was outwardly happy. But something must have been ticking away in his head and heart. Voices in the static hungering for a moment's silence to say: *Remember this, Cal, ole buddy, ole pal? Did you really think you could outrun it?*

Six years after Lydia's death—to the very day—Calvin set fire to their house on the hill. It was empty, its occupants having defaulted on the mortgage. Calvin was found on the scene with multiple stab wounds to his chest and abdomen. The house burnt to the ground and Calvin nearly died from blood loss. He'd stabbed himself. That was the most terrible part. A knife was found on the scene: the same one that had previously sat in his own kitchen cupboard.

Calvin couldn't recall doing any of it—not touching the flame to the house, not harming himself. What he did remember was being attacked by two men, who'd stabbed him with wicked knives. When questioned about where this had happened or who the men were, Calvin could not furnish a detailed reply.

"It was dark," was all he said. "This cold liquid darkness. I remember the knives flashing. They looked like darting fish."

Calvin was committed to psychiatric care. Doctors picked at the edges of the events that they realized must still exist in a recessed chamber of Calvin's mind, but by then the rift had closed. Ultimately, they declared there was no way to fix Calvin. His mind was incapable of grasping the fact that it had been broken. He wasn't a menace to the public. He might be a menace to himself, but that was no crime. Uncle C was released, and everyone hoped that would be the end of it.

But the mind is a truth-seeking organ. To use that old cliché about our hearts, it wants what it wants.

Mom drank off the dregs of her cocoa. She had poured in a few more belts of whisky while telling her story. Fatigued rings encircled her eyes.

"We hoped after burning the house, that'd be it. Nothing left, right? No physical reminders of . . . Your uncle was out of the psychiatric clinic. He was spacey, sure, but that was your uncle after the incident. That's the man you know, isn't it—spacey Uncle C."

I could only vaguely recall my uncle's absence, the time he must've spent in the psych ward. I had been three or four. My folks told me he'd gone on a long trip, "to find himself." Which was true in its way. Everything they'd told me was vaguely true, in much the same way Uncle C's understanding of his own history was true—true because they each needed it to be.

"But the house was still there, right?" Mom wiped her eyes, staring into her mug. "Burnt, but there. The car, too. They tore the old bridge down but the damn car was still there, at the bottom of the lake. Nobody dredged the oxbow. Reminders all over this damn city."

A story I'd heard about honeybees popped into my mind. We'd learned about them in science class that fall. Bees secrete a "footprint pheromone"; when they find flowers packed with pollen, they leave an invisible marker on the petals so they can find their way back. Maybe that's how it had been with my uncle: he'd returned to these spots without knowing why, compelled by a gnawing need. Could our summer

Craig Davidson

Ghost Club have gradually turned into his footprint pheromone? The car in the lake, the house, the grave-yard where his wife's marker sat. Signposts marking his way back into the past.

"Can you tell if Uncle C has remembered any of it?" I asked Mom.

"I don't think so. But it's impossible to know for sure."

I wondered at the effort it must've taken my mother and father and Lex and others to keep this secret. Dancing inches from calamity, accepting Uncle C's reworking of his own past as truth, never invoking names or events for fear they'd open some terrible door. But it was even harder to grapple with my uncle's loss—not only of his wife and unborn child, but the fact he'd never grieved them. There were two war-ring entities inside Calvin: one part sharked relent-lessly towards the truth while the other fled fearfully, stashing that truth in shadowed cubbies of his brain where some truths were best kept.

"We couldn't tell him what happened," my father told me. "The idea of doing that went out of play the night the house went up and . . . your uncle stabbed himself, Jake. To try to end your life that way indi-cates an extreme level of self-hate. Your uncle has no reason to hate himself. He's just a stranger to himself, that's all."

The clock counted off the seconds in harsh ticks. Finally, Mom spoke again.

"I'll tell you one last story, Jake. When you were born, I lost a lot of blood. You had a big head. So much that they had to put blood back into me—a transfusion." Seeing my alarm, she made a calming gesture. "The doctors gave me medicine to make me sleep. When I woke, your uncle was there in the recovery room . . . and he was pushing my blood back in. They'd put tubes in my arms. Your uncle was at the bedside with a tube in his hands, squeezing the blood back up it, like how you squeeze the toothpaste from the bottom of the tube. Trying to push it back into me."

She looked at me as if hoping that this story, a little picture-window into her brother's heart, would explain her own actions. "I love my brother, Jake. I keep his secret because to do anything else might wreck him. Your father helps me keep it because he loves me."

"I love Cal, too," my father said, sounding wounded.

My mother squeezed my hand. "I've got a favour to ask, Jake. One day he may turn a corner. But until that day, I need you to promise to keep the secret too."

7.

ALL HALLOWS' EVE

Many people believe our memories are unchanging. This belief even informs the way we talk about them: we say that our minds capture images like a camera snapshot before storing them in the vast filing cabinet of our brains. We use corporeal things—photographs, cabinets—to describe a mental process that is, in fact, in a constant state of flux. The biologist Gerald Edelman wrote that "memory is more like the melting and refreezing of a glacier than it is like an inscription on a rock." Our memories change over time. Some of this change comes through aging. But a much greater part of the change has to do with how we *want* to remember. The more distant a memory becomes, the more our minds manipulate it. The reasons for this are multiple, but often render down to: I want to remember myself, my own history and the people I care for in this specific way. So, our brains oblige.

Memory is a funny thing. People always say that.

But is it? *Funny*, I mean?

Think about this story. Consider its teller.

What follows is an account, as I choose to remember it, of my twelfth year on this planet—the summer of the Saturday Night Ghost Club. . . .

You see, I love my uncle. Even more now than I did that summer. Everyone loves my uncle. And love is the great influencer, isn't it? We will move mountains, shift space and time, for love.

Everything I've told you is true. Every word of it.

But you must know this, too: I *want* it to be true. Everything in me wants that.

For my uncle. But also for the Yellowbirds. For Lexington. For my folks. For me. For the sake of who we were back then, and to make peace with who we've become now, with all our needful ghosts.

Reality never changes. Only our recollections of it do. Whenever a moment passes, we pass along with it into the realm of memory. And in that realm, geometries change. Contours shift, shades lighten, objectivities dissolve. Memory becomes what we need it to be.

i.

"Jake Baker, come ooooon down! You're the next contestant on *The Price Is Right*!"

Halloween was Uncle C's undisputed all-time favourite night, and that year he decided to go as Bob Barker. He'd shellacked himself with bronzing cream, bought an abrasively blue wide-lapelled suit at the Goodwill, dyed his hair platinum blond and, most crucially, he had somehow laid his hands on one of Barker's signature skinny microphones. The funniest part was that the microphone wasn't plugged in. The frayed cord hung down near my uncle's ankles.

A month had passed since he'd told me the legend of Black Agnes at the graveyard. My folks had been monitoring him—a lot of "I was in the area" pop-ins at his apartment and the Occultorium—but he appeared to be fine. Buoyant, even. The cycle, if that's what it was, had ended. The pheromone trace had run cold for now.

"Now, what do you do for a living?" he asked, sticking the microphone in my face.

As I was dressed as a vampire, I answered as Dracula. "I suck zee blood of zee innocents. Uh, *blah*."

Uncle C gave my shoulder a conciliatory pat. "Rough gig, rough gig."

We were at my house, getting ready to go trick-or-treating. Mom lit a tea candle and set it inside the jack-o'-lantern on the front step. I'd carved it, my first ever attempt, and it was fairly basic, with mismatched triangle eyes and a block for a mouth. My mother cooked some spaghetti and dyed it green, draping it over the pumpkin like hair for a suitably ghoulish effect.

Dad came out of the kitchen and threw an arm around Mom's shoulder. "You two ought to get out there," he said to my uncle and me, "before all the top-shelf candy's spoken for."

"Who are you dressed as tonight, Sam?" my uncle asked.

"Will you accept Haggard Businessman?"

The sidewalks were awash with pirates and witches and werewolves, the very air infused with magic, mystery and the bleeding edge of menace. Anything was possible on the one night when ghosts walked amongst the living. We hit the corner of Harvard and Delisle. Billy waited for us against a lamppost. He had a fake walrus moustache affixed with spirit gum, a pair of thrift-store spectacles and an old worsted-wool suit.

I had no clue who he was dressed as, but my uncle cried, "It's Charles Fort, author of *The Book of the Damned.*" He clapped Billy on the back. "Good show, old sport. Positively topping!"

We ramped into full-tilt trick-or-treat mode. After a few blocks, I was sweating and my sack was getting full. We had stopped to catch our breath when someone rode up with a pumpkin on their head.

"Hey, bozos," Dove said, pulling the jack-o'-lantern off.

"Where'd you get that?" my uncle wanted to know.

"Some loser's house. I cut a hole in the bottom. Pretty cool, uh?"

My uncle crossed his arms. "That's theft, Dove."

She tucked the pumpkin under her arm the way spacemen do their helmets. "They had a bunch. They'll never miss it."

She put the pumpkin in her bike basket and rode along beside us. There was a pumpkin seed in her hair. We turned down Sarah Court, not hurrying now, enjoying the night. Kids drifted in and out of pockets of shadow between the street lights. I spotted Percy Elkins, walking alone dressed as an executioner, dragging a plastic axe along the sidewalk.

At Janet Templeton's house, I was shocked when Lex answered the door. Jan came up behind him, hugging him round the waist. Evidently Janet had turfed gloomy Stan Rowe and taken Lex back. As the years wore on, I'd hear more about Lex through my uncle. He and Janet never had kids but their house was crammed with cats—calicos and Siameses and Maine Coons. And although he was romantically satisfied, Lex's string of questionable business decisions continued. After letting the lease expire on So Beta! he opened a camera shop to serve Cataract City's tourist clientele. That shop's name? Polaroid Dreams.

We waved goodbye to Lex and Janet and returned to the sidewalk. Dove plucked a Tootsie Roll out of my bag, unwrapped it and popped it in her mouth.

"Boys, it's been a slice, but this is where I leave you."

"Go put that pumpkin back," my uncle told her.

Dove stuck her tongue out at him. "Who spayed or neutered you today?"

She rode down the sidewalk, turned towards the shadow side of the street and melted into darkness. I didn't know it then, but after that night, I'd see less and less of Dove. She began to dabble with things best left un-dabbled with. It was like Mrs. Yellowbird said: Dove lived as suns do. She seemed happiest in that heat. But lately things have been looking up for her. Billy tells me she's down in San Francisco, still the last safe haven for a wild child. She's got a new girlfriend. They live in a bohemian loft that works on a barter system. She's a sculptor, a talent that had long lain dormant. Billy says the pieces just flow out of her. Her latest was called *Never Wake the Dreamer*, and was bought by a Silicon Valley entrepreneur. Dove is happy, and if she ever needs that hand to hold while slipping into the long dark, hey, of course I'll be there.

Billy and I hotfooted it for another block and a half. Once our bags were bulging we sat on a bus bench inventorying our hauls while Uncle C kept up the patter. "Looks like Dracula's angling to swap a Mars bar for a pack of Skittles—would you like to keep that showcase, unlamented genius Charles Fort, or go for showcase number two?"

Billy and I would continue to be thick as thieves, in high school, in university and to this day. Billy would be our high school's star wide receiver. He shot up nearly half a foot in tenth grade, and our coach marvelled at his Krazy Glue fingertips. He earned a scholarship to play at a university up north and I went with him. We shared a dorm room, then a little two-bedroom apartment off-campus. Eventually I found my calling and moved south to pursue a medical degree. After graduating, Billy bounced around the CFL: Ottawa, Saskatchewan and finally Toronto, where I was then living. He blew out his knee on a slant route in his seventh season, retired, and moved back to Slave Lake to do outreach work. I miss the hell out of that guy.

That Halloween, my uncle and I said our goodbyes to Billy, and he set off home. We moved west, just the two of us, walking without speaking, only the whisper of our shoes and the brush of Uncle C's microphone cord on the sidewalk. He looked good, though that may have been the bronzer. Still, I sensed he was happy—my uncle had no emotional firewall, and you could read his face as easily as the hands on a clock.

ii.

Whenever I'm in town, I stop by the Occultorium, which still sits on the corner of Walnut and Ellen, spitting distance from Clifton Hill. You're welcome to pop in yourself, stock up on shrunken heads and Haitian curse amulets. If so, you might spy the Bat Phone through the beaded curtain at the back. It doesn't ring these days. *Truth seeking is a young man's game*, my uncle said the day he unplugged it. The phone remains in its place of privilege, though, and I like to imagine that my uncle's eyes drift to it from time to time, half-expecting it to ring—*that* would be one call he'd have to answer. I often wonder what became of Uncle C's network of cranks and conspiracy theorists. Dark Heshie, the Venomed Voice, the

Watcher. People the world had broken in some ineffable way, the same way my uncle had been broken, the same way we all end up a bit broken—a collection of small hurts, hairline cracks in the foundation—who were only looking for something to give their lives meaning, hope, or at least help deal with the confusion. Some of us find it in faith, some in science and some in the lightless places between those pole stars.

Uncle C never married again. Never had a child. Which was tragic, because he would have made a great father. He did adopt a black Lab, Skeptic, who suits his personality. He and Skeptic come over for Sunday dinners at my folks' house, where the conversation will sometimes ping on a topic best left buried and a pall settles over the table . . . but never for long. They're all good at directing their boat into cheerier waters, whether consciously or not.

"I can't believe our Jake grew up to be a doctor," Calvin might say. "A healer of men!"

Sometimes I fall into thinking about my uncle in the context of fate, fairness, the transforming forces that haunt our lives. I don't know why that awfulness befell his family. All I can say is that evil exists in this world, and it has to touch somebody. Plus, evil is chicken-gutted. It finds the weakest spots between the beams. The uncle I've known all my life is not the same man he was before I came along. Grief and loss crushed him into a shape unrecognizable to his prior self.

The other thing I know is that my uncle will never understand his own strength. It was this strength he must have called upon during those nights he spent in the basement of the Occultorium with the beat of the falls pulsing against the fieldstone walls like a heartbeat; isolated under the light of a bare bulb with the spirit phone, keying the name of a woman he'd never known on the Speak & Spell.

L-Y-D-I-A

I imagine the machine issuing its deep-space crackle as he sent those five letters into the ether like a note in a bottle, over the curvature of the earth, her name floating between worlds known and worlds only guessed at, up to the Super-Sargasso—that vast dark thing poised like a crow over the moon—my uncle's breath locked behind his ribs as he waited, wondering why this meant so much to him. Did a voice drift through the silver horn one of those nights, soft as a lover's breath on the nape of his neck?

He must have needed strength on those other nights when he sat bolt upright in bed with the remnant of a dream draining from his brainpan: the vision of a woman and the house they shared atop a hill. His happiness must have curdled into a feeling of immense loss at the realization it was only a dream, that the life behind his eyelids wasn't his own and never had been. . . . Perhaps he tried to fasten the dream in his mind, enjoy it a heartbeat longer, but something was stealthily pulling it away from him—and on the next beat it was gone.

On that long-ago Halloween night, I took my uncle's hand: a boy-vampire and a game-show host walking hand in hand through the long dark of Cataract City. Years later, we would walk these same streets with Skeptic and my son Nicholas, who was dressed as a ghost in a plain bedsheet with eye-holes cut in it. My son was between us, holding our hands. And Uncle C, whom by then I called Cal, knelt beside his great-nephew and peered into the boy's eyes through those holes.

"Nicholas, did I ever tell you that there are friendly ghosts? Right here in our fair city, yes! They live in the space between waking and dream, and if we know where to look, we can spot them. Just before you fall asleep, you'll see a shimmering."

Skeptic issued a soft bark, as if in agreement. Nicholas looked at me, his eyes expressing curiosity but no fear, and I offered a wry smile to let him know that hey, maybe there *are* ghosts, but he shouldn't swallow everything his great-uncle says.

"Do not be alarmed, my boy, and don't ever be afraid. These ghosts mean no harm. They are spirits who have lost their way. They wander the great unknown in search of peace, and wish to guide us to safety whenever we find ourselves in danger. But you have to believe. Only then will they reveal themselves to you."

At this, Calvin kissed my son on the nose, his lips pressed to the sheet.

"And that," he said, "is why I'll always believe in ghosts."

ACKNOWLEDGEMENTS

First, thanks to my mother and father.

Let's talk about Mom and Dad a bit.

I tend to be a bit of a magpie, collecting bits and pieces of ephemera, life stories and such, to cobble together my nest of a novel. I take my own experiences and those of others and spin them through a fictional filter, as do many writers. So, are Cecelia and Sam Baker in this novel my Mom and Dad? No, not exactly. But are they kind of alike? Sure they are.

My mother and father didn't meet outside the Bonny in Niagara Falls. They met at the Speakeasy, a bar that used to sit on the corner of Bathurst and Bloor in Toronto. As my mother says, she first saw my father under a table there. As my father says, he first saw my mother dancing on top of that same table. Their eyes met, sparks flew, etcetera.

Dad was starting his career as a banker. Mom was finishing nursing school. They began to date. But Dad preferred more sedate activities than Mom. Going to movies, bars. Mom loved dancing, craved action. They didn't jibe. Mom dumped Dad: *Sorry, Donald, but this just isn't working.*

Dad pined for Mom like only a lovelorn young man can. And then—and this always gets me—he went out and signed up for dancing lessons from a Greek lady on the Danforth. Mastered the rhumba, the fox-trot, whatever the hot dance of the day was . . . the Bop? We Davidsons are notoriously poor dancers. Our hips are fused to our spines, preventing any kind of graceful movement. But damned if Dad didn't try. Then he bought a new (used) car, a '67 Pontiac, and went a-courting. Wonder of wonders, Mom took him back. They went dancing. Dad was pretty bad, but Mom appreciated the attempt. They got married, and a few years later I came along.

So, thanks Mom and Dad. Thanks, Dad, for getting those dance lessons. Thanks, Mom, for forcing Dad out of his safe zone. Thanks to you both, eternally, for all the support and love you've given me through the years. As I write somewhere in this book, "Kids never quite love their parents as much as their parents love them." It's almost impossible to do so, I think. I love my son more than he's capable of loving me. But I think that if you're a good, constant, ever-caring parent, in time that wheel does come around.

Thanks as always to my wife, Colleen, and our son, Nicholas. Always, always.

This book started out as a PhD thesis. I'd like to thank my advisor, Dr. Richard House, and Dr. Luke Kennard, Dr. Ruth Gilligan, Dr. Dan Vyleta and Dr. Paul McDonald for their thoughtful edits and wisdom in the developing stages of this novel during my stint at the University of Birmingham.

Thanks to my bud Sam Pane, whose audio documentary on the Screaming Tunnels brought me back to that time in my life when such places enthralled and terrified me in equal measure.

Thanks to Stephen King, John Bellairs, Wilson Rawls, Judy Blume, and all the writers I was reading at the age Jake is in this novel. I owe each of them a huge debt of influence.

Thanks as always to my agent, Kirby Kim, who puts up with all my writerly nonsense and hand-wringing with good cheer and grace. Appreciate it, mon frere.

Finally, huge thanks to my editor, Lynn Henry. I continually foist an ungainly mess of a manuscript on you, and somehow you manage to spin gold out of it. How do you do it? You are a meddler in the dark arts, I suspect. Calvin probably has your name in one of his spiral-bound notebooks. Yet, at the peril of your everlasting soul, you continue to make my work so much better. I am eternally grateful.

CRAIG DAVIDSON was born in Toronto and grew up in St. Catharines, Ontario. He has published four previous books of literary fiction, including *Rust and Bone*, which was made into a Golden Globe-nominated film; and *Cataract City*, which was shortlisted for the Scotiabank Giller Prize and the Trillium Book Prize, and was a national bestseller. His memoir, *Precious Cargo: My Year Driving the Kids on School Bus 3077*, also a bestseller, was shortlisted for Canada Reads. Craig Davidson has published several popular horror novels under the name Nick Cutter. He lives in Toronto, Canada, with his wife and son.